Also By Liliana Rhodes

His Every Whim
His Every Whim, Part 1
His One Desire, Part 2
His Simple Wish, Part 3
His True Fortune, Part 4
The Billionaire's Whim - Boxed Set

Canyon Cove Billionaires
Playing Games
No Regrets
Second Chance

Made Man Trilogy
Soldier
Capo
Boss
Made Man Dante - Boxed Set

Made Man Novels
Made Man Sonny

The Crane Curse Trilogy
Charming the Alpha
Resisting the Alpha
Needing the Alpha
The Crane Curse Trilogy Boxed Set

Wolf at Her Door

A CANYON COVE NOVEL

Liliana Rhodes

Published by
Jaded Speck Publishing
5042 Wilshire Blvd #30861
Los Angeles, CA 90036

No Regrets
A Canyon Cove Novel
Copyright © 2015 by Liliana Rhodes
Cover by CT Cover Designs

ISBN 978-1-939918-05-5

This book is a work of fiction. The names, characters, places, and incidents are products of the writer's imagination or have been used fictitiously and are not to be construed as real. Any resemblance to persons, living or dead, actual events, locales or organizations is entirely coincidental.

All rights reserved. No part of this book may be reproduced, scanned, or distributed in any manner whatsoever without written permission from the author except in the case of brief quotation embodied in critical articles and reviews.

Dedication

To my son.

Chapter One

Deborah

The sun beat down, barely giving any escape. Even under the trees there was no relief. Walking past the old brick campus buildings I had my classes in, I wondered why I had never felt so much heat radiating off the bricks before. Up ahead in the clearing, students and school administrators milled about, waiting. Just beyond them were rows of white wooden chairs facing a long stage.

As I approached the small crowd of people in their caps and gowns, I wished I thought to bring my sunglasses. Squinting as I looked around, I slipped the black silky material of my graduation gown on like a coat over the tan jeans and cotton button down shirt I wore, grateful to not have to mess up my chin-length bob.

I hoped to look casual, like I didn't care about graduation, but the truth was I cared much more than I wanted to admit. Zipping the gown up the front and then draping the red honors sash over my shoulders, I looked like all the other Canyon Cove University graduates. Except maybe a little rounder and definitely shorter.

My weight had been a sensitive issue since my neighbor Patty asked me why I was so fat. I was four at the time and at my chubbiest. I didn't know what fat was, but by the tone of her voice, I knew it was a bad thing. I ran home crying and told my grandmother what happened.

Of course Grandma tried to make me feel better by saying we all came in different shapes and sizes, but it didn't matter. The damage had been done. Since then, I was always aware of how much larger I was compared to others. I knew sometimes it was all in my head, but I couldn't help it. It was like Patty had permanently taken up residence in my head.

Luckily for me, the older I got, the less I cared about what others thought. Sometime in high school when I really began caring about clothes, I realized how unfair it was that big girls couldn't dress cute.

It was around that time that I would go shopping with my girlfriends at the mall and while they had endless stores to choose from, I was lucky to have one. Usually that one store only carried conservative old lady clothes that I was far from wearing as a teen. I was a young girl, I didn't want to dress like my grandma. That was when I started making my own clothes.

As I walked around, I looked at the faces of the other graduates, hoping to find someone familiar. I didn't recognize anyone. Between working a couple of jobs and school, I didn't have much of a social life. Watching them hug and smile at each other, I felt really out of place, like I missed out on something. It didn't help that at twenty-five, they were younger than me by a few years. *Shit, why am I here?*

"Deborah! Deborah Hansen!"

Recognizing Ashley Boone's voice, I turned around, breathing a sigh of relief that I wasn't completely alone but thinking it odd to see her here. Ashley had been my boss at the Winslow Museum for Motion Pictures and was the sweetest person ever. She even offered me her job when she decided to become a stay at home mom. I was happy to call Ashley my friend.

"Ashley! What are you doing here?" I asked as I walked towards her. Looking beautiful as usual with her long dark hair, pouty lips, and an orange print sundress that hugged her curves, Ashley held her infant son Jacob. I was reminded of paintings of the Madonna and child. "Wait, that didn't come out right," I said, laughing. "I'm glad to see you, but how did you know? I didn't tell you about this."

She laughed as she hugged me. "I know you better than you think," she said as she grinned at me. "You mentioned graduating this semester so I looked up the date. I knew you wouldn't miss walking."

"You're right, but I really don't know why I'm here. This is stupid. I don't even know anyone here, and I don't have anyone here, either. Well, I didn't until you came."

"You should be happy, Deborah. You're finally graduating! You should walk and be proud! You'll never get another chance to do this."

"I know. That's the only reason I'm here. I don't want to look back and regret the things I didn't do. There have been so many things in my life...I almost didn't finish school, but I knew I'd regret that, too. Before my grandma died, she said life was too short to regret the things you didn't do.

She had so many regrets. She made me promise I'd follow my heart and never regret anything."

"She sounds like she was a wise, wonderful woman."

"She was something else, that's for sure," I said, laughing as I remembered her spunkiness. "I miss her. You know, she raised me. I couldn't ask for a better life growing up even though we had no money. Speaking of money, where's Mr. Billionaire?"

"He'll be here later to pick up the baby for his nap. Then you and I are going to *Joyeux*. Joshua feels awful about not calling you and demanded I bring you by his shop so he could finally meet you in person."

"That sounds great!"

"Graduates," a woman's voice called out over the crowd. "Please line up. The procession will begin shortly."

"I'll meet you back here when it's over," Ashley said. "Go line up! Make your grandma even prouder than I'm sure she already is."

Ashley gave me a big hug, careful to not disturb Jacob, who was sleeping. Smiling sheepishly at her, I felt tears fill my eyes and quickly blinked, trying to stop them from falling. It was useless though, so I blotted the corners of my eyes with my fingertips, trying to save my makeup.

"Dammit Ash, you made me cry! I'll look like a raccoon accepting my diploma," I joked, hoping to make my tears stop. "Please, go so you can get a seat. I'd feel awful if you had to stand in this heat the entire time."

As Ashley left, I found my spot in line with the other H's. Looking around at my fellow graduates, I straightened my honors sash and looked up through the tall trees at the cloudless sky.

This is for you, Grandma, I thought. *I really hope you're up there watching.* I looked down at the ground. *Or watching from down there where you always said you'd be.*

As I laughed to myself, Pomp and Circumstance played and the long procession walked under the famed wrought iron arch of the university and towards the stage set up on the grassy campus plaza. I continued to think about my grandma as I walked, remembering her wicked sense of humor and all the things she taught me about life.

As I sat on a wooden folding chair surrounded by a sea full of strangers, the heat of the black graduation cap and gown started to get to me. What I wouldn't do for a breeze or even a little rain. I knew I should've stayed home.

Suddenly the bright sun slipped behind a small dark cloud and it began to rain. Some people ran for cover. Most of the graduates stayed in their seats, grateful for the break in the heat. I laughed and looked back up at the sky. *Ah-ha! I knew you'd be up there! Thanks, Grandma.*

Chapter Two

Deborah

Shortly after receiving my diploma, the steady drizzle became a downpour. I spotted Ashley near the walkway just beyond the graduation arch, kissing Jacob on the forehead as she handed him to a smiling Xander, who held an umbrella.

Xander was the perfect handsome complement to Ashley. Together, they looked like they had just stepped out of a magazine. With his perfectly trimmed beard and hair a little on the longer side, I could see why Ashley fell for him. And to watch how he looked at her, you could see the intense love in his eyes. In both their eyes, really.

I waved to them as I headed towards my car. They looked so happy. I couldn't help it. For a brief second, I was jealous. It wasn't that I wanted a family or even a husband. I didn't even want to be bothered with a boyfriend right now. The last thing I needed was that kind of distraction. It's just that since Grandma died, there were times I felt really alone.

"That was a beautiful ceremony, Deb," Ashley said once she caught up with me.

"Yeah, I guess it wasn't that bad. Thankfully the rain made them cut it short."

"We can take my car. It's in the lot across the street. Are you parked there, too?"

"Ha, no. I popped all the money I had into the meter and hoped I wouldn't get a ticket," I said as I pointed to the navy four-door piece of shit that used to be my grandmother's car. "I need to take my car, I'm sure the meter's up. How about if I follow you to Joshua's?"

"Sure, I'll pull around to meet you," she said before heading towards the parking lot.

I unlocked my car and slipped in behind the steering wheel, throwing the cap and gown onto the seat beside me. Turning the key in the ignition, I felt my stomach drop when nothing happened. The car was silent.

"Shit! Not now! No, not now!" I yelled as I turned the key again. But the only sound I heard was the click of my keys against the console. "Please, please, please start!" As Ashley pulled up next to me in her beautiful, expensive SUV, I shook my head and begged. "Not in front of her. Please start. Don't make her feel sorry for me."

Pulling the key out then shoving it back into the ignition and twisting it hard, the car suddenly came to life. I breathed a sigh of relief before pulling out into traffic behind Ashley.

After a quick drive on the freeway, we got off an exit that brought us closer to the center of the city of Canyon Cove. As we stopped at a red light, I looked over at the car stopped beside mine in the next lane. It was a shiny black sports coupe, and I slowly realized I knew the car. *Doug? It couldn't be...could it?*

Doug Murray was my last boyfriend and at almost a year, my longest relationship. We met the first year of college and had an immediate attraction to each other. He played lacrosse and had a laid back style I found irresistible. With spiky brown hair and dimples in his cheeks when he smiled, every girl turned their heads to look when Doug entered the room.

Surprised to see him, I stared until Doug turned and looked back at me. I smiled and waved, but I could see by his face that he didn't know who I was. As recognition slowly filled his face, he covered his mouth with one hand, pointed at me with the other, and laughed.

The traffic light couldn't change fast enough. I knew I was heavier than the last time he saw me, but his laughter felt like he reached into my chest and yanked my heart out and stomped on it. Wishing I could say something to him to put him in his place, I lifted my hand up and extended my middle finger at him as the light turned green.

When Ashley and I reached the parking lot of Fashion Plaza, I stepped out of my car, still shaken up by Doug's mocking.

"You alright? You don't look so good." Ashley said as we followed the path from the parking lot into the shopping area.

"Yes, I'm fine," I said then sighed. "No, I'm really not. It's my ex. I just saw him."

"When? Now? What happened?"

"Yeah, just now. At the traffic light. It's just so odd because he was being such an ass, but when we were together, he really wasn't. He was actually really sweet. We even stayed friends for a while afterwards, but I guess we lost touch."

"Sounds like you're leaving something out."

"Yeah, I guess I ignored the obvious. I feel bad about that," I said as I thought about the past. "Doug went to college full time so he graduated a couple of years ago. It was around that time that my grandmother took a turn for the worse. Between that and all the time I was spending with Doug while he decided what to do with his degree, my grades started to suffer.

"I guess I should've been more honest with Doug, but I was so upset about my grandma that I shut down. I broke up with Doug and we decided to stay friends. He'd invite me over and we'd hang out. It was nice.

"I should've seen the signs though. I don't think he was over me. Maybe he thought if we stayed friends we'd get back together. I really don't know, he never said anything." I thought quietly for a moment before continuing. "I remember one day he played a song and told me to listen to the end, that those lyrics really made him think of me. Maybe I should've paid more attention."

"What did it say?"

"Something about how he knew I would be the star in another person's sky and why couldn't it be his." I shook my head as I realized what he was saying then. "Eventually he stopped returning my calls. That was about a year ago." My voice trailed off as I mentally kicked myself. "Boy, am I dense."

"No Deb, you said it yourself, you were going through a lot. Don't be so hard on yourself. He was an asshole for what he just did. Forget about him and just focus on meeting Joshua. You'll love him, he's great."

Entering the store, all my worries slipped away. Ashley continued to talk, but I barely heard her. Mannequins modeled some of the most fashion-forward styles I had seen not only in Canyon Cove but even on the cover of Vogue. *Joyeux* was everything I dreamed about for myself.

Ashley touching my arm brought me back to reality, and I followed her gaze towards the back of the store where she exchanged waves with an attractive man I recognized as Joshua Cane. With his brown hair perfectly slicked back, just a hint of stubble on his cheek, and his welcoming smile, he looked just as perfect as he did when he was featured in magazines.

Standing beside him was a nervous young woman with flaxen hair who looked like she hadn't eaten in years. After giving instructions to her, he then snapped his fingers at her twin. It wasn't until the two women were running around doing his bidding that he sauntered over to us, wearing a dark pair of almost too tight jeans and a tucked-in button shirt in a bronze print that accentuated his tanned skin.

"Ashley, you gorgeous thing you," he said before kissing her on both cheeks. "I have some fabulous new items for you. My assistant Corrie will escort you to the dressing room where everything's waiting. If you need anything, she will be at your beck and call."

"Well, aren't you just all business?" Ashley teased him. "Joshua, this is Deborah--"

"Of course it is, darling." He extended his hand in my direction and I shook it. "I recognize her from the University newspaper. Did you know she took first place in ready-to-wear?"

"Really? I had no idea! Why didn't you tell me?" Ashley asked me.

"It's not a big deal. I mean of course I was thrilled to win, but..." I didn't know what else to say without talking about how it was just a school competition with so many categories that everyone won something. Even if I did think I won the best category, I thought there were others with more creative designs.

"But you don't think you really deserved it, do you?" Joshua said.

"No, I...I worked hard for it. I knew my work spoke for itself and deserved to win, I just..." *Didn't think I should win* is what I thought, but those words I knew were best kept to myself.

"Corrie, please take Mrs. Boone to try on my fall collection," Joshua called out to one of the women before he turned back to Ashley. "We need to catch up sometime and I'd love to see that adorable baby of yours, but today is business. I want to focus my attention on this talented designer you've brought me."

"Sure, just call me whenever you want to come by," she said before following Corrie to the dressing rooms.

"Come with me, I'm sure Carrie has everything under control in the store."

"Carrie? I thought her name was Corrie," I said.

"Carrie is my other assistant. They're twins. Because you know, my life isn't complicated enough without having to figure out whether I'm seeing double or just looking at them."

He laughed as I followed him to a quiet corner of the store, blocked from direct view by Asian inspired silk screens depicting a serene water garden. His work area consisted of a long work table, a sewing machine, a high end HP tablet/laptop combo that sat on a small desk, a dress form for fittings, and a corner filled with yards upon yards of fabric.

"Wow, this is exactly the kind of place I want to have one day," I said as I looked at his sketches that were pinned on the wall.

"I'm sure you will one day. From what I've seen, you are very talented."

"Thanks, but--"

"But nothing. Own that. You are talented, young lady, don't ever forget that. If you have a dream, you have to go for it. Remember, no one is going to just give you what you want, you have to make your dreams happen."

I nodded as his words sunk into me. "You're right. That's why I pushed myself to finish school and graduate. I could've stopped so many times and just given up."

"Listen, Deborah. I never do this, but I loved what I saw and we do share an alma mater. There's a lot I can teach you about running your own brand. I'd like to offer you a job here as my assistant."

"Assistant? Like Corrie and Carrie? Thanks, but I really don't think so."

"No, no, no. Trust me, I know what you're thinking. Those two are assistants in that they help me take care of customers. I'm offering you the chance to design with me."

"Wow, Joshua. I didn't expect this. But I really don't know, I need to think about it, and I want to weigh all my options now that I've graduated. I'm not saying I wouldn't want to work with you. The experience would be amazing. I just don't want to jump into anything and right now my head is spinning. I need time to think."

"Of course. I don't want you to rush into it, either. Listen, speaking of options, I have a friend who works over in HR at Hargrove's."

"The high-end department store? I really don't want to work retail. I don't see how that'll help me become a designer."

"Hear me out. In Canyon Cove, there aren't many options and this is a good one. Hargrove's has an employee only fashion design contest every year. The winner gets to feature their collection in the store. If Hargrove's feels the collection is strong enough, they'll even send the designer to Fashion Week."

"For real? How did I not know about this?"

"It's one of their best kept secrets. I wish they had something like this when I graduated," he said as he smiled at me. "You take your time and think about my offer. If you break my heart I'll understand, but at least consider Hargrove's. I'll put in a good word and make sure you're not just stocking shelves all day. Think about it and give me a call, okay? Here's LuAnne's number if you decide to go that route," he said as he wrote down a phone number on a small piece of paper.

"Thanks, Joshua. You'll hear from me one way or the other. Thank you for everything."

"Anytime. Us designers have to stick together, you know. I'm more than happy to help."

***

Finally getting home, I felt the day catch up with me as I collapsed onto the old brown and tan polyester couch that doubled as my bed. I dropped my stack of mail onto the kitchen table without looking at it. I didn't have to sort through them to know they were bills. If it had my name on it, they were looking for money.

As I kicked off my shoes, one of the envelopes caught my eye. It was a little longer than my credit card bills and looked thin. I picked it up and held it up to the light, afraid to open it.

"Please don't be what I think this is," I said, annoyed as I examined the envelope. "Are you kidding me? I just came from graduation!" I said.

Opening it, I felt my stomach sink and slowly turn. It was exactly what I feared--my student loans were already asking for payment.

Quietly slipping out of my closet, my orange and white cat hopped onto an arm of the couch and started purring. I rescued Mousetrap from a shelter after his owner kicked him out, annoyed that he betrayed his name and what she considered his sole purpose in life. Trap was not only the laziest cat I have ever met, but I was sure he'd run in the other direction if he ever saw a mouse. In other words, Trap and I had a lot in common.

"Shit Trap, talk about bad timing" I said loudly as I fell back onto the couch, wishing I hadn't gotten up to check that letter. "I thought I had a few months before they wanted anything. Maybe I should call Drake Winslow and see if Ashley's job is still open. I could use that kind of money. Maybe I shouldn't have turned it down."

Trap meowed his reply. His "talking" was the reason I took him home. I never planned on adopting a pet, but next thing I knew Trap was talking to me from a cage as I walked past a pet adoption fair. Figuring it was never too early to fulfill my destiny as the crazy cat lady, I adopted him. Besides, I spent way too much time talking to myself. Trap made me seem a little less wacky.

"No? No regrets? When you're right, you're right, Trap," I said as I scratched his neck.

Looking around my small studio apartment, I knew I couldn't scale down any further. Any smaller and I would be living in a closet or a nice refrigerator box. Mentally going through my poor excuse of a budget, I knew it was only a matter of time before I wouldn't be able to pay rent. I needed a job now, but I really wanted to pursue my dream. If I didn't do that now, I didn't know when I'd have the chance to. There would never be a perfect time.

As I thought about my talk with Joshua, I considered taking him up on his offer of working at *Joyeux*. I knew he'd let me help design, but it would be under his name, not mine. And since we both designed for plus size as well as smaller sizes, I knew it would be hard for me to really stand out. Joshua was such a talented designer, my work couldn't compare to his.

I pulled out the piece of paper he gave me and turned it over between my fingers. Hargrove's was *the* high end department store, actually it was considered a fine department store. That's how fancy it was. But I really didn't want a retail job. They were a lot of work for not much pay. I wanted to design, to create fashion. Not sell what was already on a hanger.

Joshua was right though, Hargrove's could be an amazing opportunity because of their Annual Designer Challenge. The chance that I could win that or even get a foot in with a buyer was tempting enough for me to ignore what working retail meant. I dialed the number Joshua gave me and crossed my fingers as I listened to the phone ring.

"Thank you for calling Hargrove's," the automated voice on the other end of the call answered. "You've reached the Human Resources department. Your call will be answered shortly."

"Human Resources, this is Joan."

"Hi, this is Deborah Hansen, I'm looking for LuAnne?"

"What is this regarding?"

"Joshua Cane suggested I give her a call."

"Oh Joshua!" she said, her voice suddenly friendly. "Yes, right away. One moment please."

"This is LuAnne," she said with a twangy accent I couldn't place. "You're friends with Josh? How is he? I need to call him."

"He's good. He said I should give you a call."

"Great, what can I help you with?"

"Well, I just graduated with a degree in Fashion Design from Canyon Cove University and I was wondering if you have any openings?"

"Everyone at Hargrove's starts on the selling floor. Are you alright with that?"

"Can I still participate in the Designer Challenge?"

"Of course you can, that's open for everyone, but the deadline is approaching," she said. "Listen, since I'm in a good mood and you're friends with Josh, I know of an opening as a tailor in the men's department. It's a busy department and while it might not be high on your list, at least it's more than just working the floor. Why don't you come in and I can tell you more about it. Is 10am good?"

"Sounds great. I'll be there," I said before hanging up and bouncing happily in my seat. "There you go, Trap! Things are turning around. Maybe now I won't have to worry about you attacking me in my sleep out of starvation."

Chapter Three

Deborah

After walking down the inconspicuous path near the parking garage entrance for Hargrove's, I entered my code into the keypad and entered the building. My first couple of days were mostly orientation and paperwork, but after that I was finally allowed on the floor.

While my title was 'tailor', I knew I wasn't much more than a glorified salesperson. The job definitely had its faults but I kept reassuring myself that it wasn't a step back, that with the right connections I could get a buyer interested in looking at my designs.

Plus there was the Annual Designer Challenge. Hargrove's was famous for its window displays along the avenue. At Christmas, people would crowd around the windows for a glimpse.

The contest gave the winning designer a collection display in the window, put the designs up for sale in all of their stores, plus the chance that Hargrove's would sponsor the collection at Paris Fashion Week. It was an exciting opportunity and the only reason I took the job.

Walking down the long hall, I looked over my outfit as I did every morning I came to work at Hargrove's since I started a week ago. Knowing how much I'd be on my feet, I wore a pair of black palazzo pants and an ivory organza blouse with ruffled sleeves and a deep v-neck. Both pieces were made by me. I tried to wear as much of my own designs as possible since I had such a hard time finding clothes that fit me properly, not just because of my shape, but because of my height.

As I walked on the store's white marble floors towards the men's department, I could already see that last night's sales team had left a mess. Dianna, the manager who trained me, was already on the floor and putting the clothing back on hangers or getting them ready for folding. Usually everyone towered over me, but she was just as short and very petite. She reminded me of a china doll with her perfect auburn waves hanging down her back. That is, she did until she turned around.

Dianna Brubaker's facial features were reminiscent of a bird. Her thin, pointed nose hooked down at the end, pointing to an equally pointy chin. Her sharp features were unfortunately accentuated by her fragile frame, which she covered up with long flowing skirts and buttoned up tops. All of it combined made her look much older than her thirty years of age.

The poor girl looked like she could get blown away at any second, and she regularly complained about it. Dianna ate constantly, always hiding food in the drawers around the register. It was another one of her tirades--no matter how much she ate, she couldn't gain any weight. I hated her for it. Not that I wanted to be that thin, but I wouldn't mind not having to consider the size of my ass when I was squeezing into a restaurant booth.

"If you ever leave the department looking like this, I swear I'll kick your ass," she said as I approached.

"Hey, I know better. Plus I'd still get stuck having to clean it up," I said as I started folding a rumpled pile of expensive polo shirts.

"Listen, I know you just started, but I need you to take care of men's alterations by yourself today. I have a new girl starting who will focus on this mess and if I don't put the fear of God into her, we'll have another Sara, who's too busy flirting to keep the place neat. Think you can handle it?"

"Of course! Alterations is why I took this position. You know I love to sew."

"Good, if you have any problems, just page me. It's usually a little slow during the day, but you never know."

I navigated my way through the clothing racks to the wide fitting room area. Hargrove's wasn't an ordinary department store. What really set them apart was the superior customer experience. For example, anyone could buy an item at Hargrove's and have it expertly tailored free of charge. Of course, a lot of the clothing we sold was out of my wallet's reach, but still, it was a nice thought.

The men's fitting area was warm with rich forest green carpeting and dark wood furniture. Towards the rear was a three-sided mirror where most fittings were done. On the right were oversized dressing rooms. I checked the rack customers used to hang the clothing they didn't want and found what I expected--it was full.

I hadn't had the pleasure of working with Sara yet, and I didn't want it. Not only had Dianna warned me enough about her, but every time I worked after her, the department looked like a tornado had gone through it.

The mess didn't bother me that much though. It gave me something to do and as long as I was busy, the day zipped by. Nothing slows a day down more than standing around waiting for customers.

Grabbing as many dress pants on hangers as I could carry, I walked over to the suit area and began fitting them back on the rack by their size. Looking through the new suit styles that came in the other day was a tall, handsome man with dark brown hair slightly parted on the side and pushed back from his forehead. He was clean-shaven and wore a black suit with a grey shirt and no tie. I couldn't take my eyes off him.

Realizing the number of pants in my arms was dwindling, I slowed down my clean up effort. I didn't want to stop staring at him. His broad shoulders tugged his suit jacket perfectly across his back and each time he pulled another suit out of the rack, I noticed the wrinkle on his sleeve where his muscles flexed.

I didn't know what came over me. I had seen handsome, sexy men before, but this one put them all to shame. I tried focusing back on putting the clothes away but then, almost as if he could feel my eyes burning a hole in him, he turned to look at me and smiled.

While I thought he was gorgeous from behind, now getting a full look at his face, I didn't have words to describe him. Beautiful? No, he wasn't a pretty boy, he was rugged and manly with a strong jawline I wanted to lick. I couldn't help but gawk, and I hoped I wasn't drooling like I imagined. He was beyond good looking, he was magnetic. My head kept coming back to calling him Sexy, Mr. Sexy.

Suddenly I imagined Mr. Sexy running on a beach in nothing but black board shorts, the white pull string at his waist tempting me as water droplets slowly dripped down his sun-kissed skin and disappearing into the fabric. *Whoa, get a hold of yourself, Deborah!* I mentally told myself.

Smiling back, I realized Mr. Sexy was still looking at me. His friendly smile changed to something different, a small, gently lopsided knowing smile, the right corner of his mouth just a little bit higher than the left. I wondered what he knew about me. *Was he reading my mind? No, that was just stupid.*

As he walked over to me, my breath caught. My first instinct was to run so I wouldn't embarrass myself, but then I heard my grandma's advice in my head--*no regrets*. I stood firmly in my spot, still holding the hangers and gazing into his approaching face as I tried to keep my eyes from traveling down the rest of Mr. Sexy's body.

He had gentle smile lines on his cheeks and at the corners of his eyes. And those eyes! Now that he was closer, I could see they were hazel with glittering green flecks. They were the warmest and most inviting eyes I had ever seen. I knew if he asked me anything at that moment, anything at all, the answer would be yes.

"Excuse me," he said as his eyes quickly found my name tag. "Deborah."

"Yes..." I responded, using the only word I was able to say and playing over his deeply intoxicating voice in my head.

"I believe you dropped something."

"Yes..." I said as his words slowly registered in my brain.

Looking down, I saw all the hangers I was holding were empty. All of the dress pants slid off and were in a pile on the floor at my feet. I had been so consumed with this man that I didn't even realize what happened.

"Shit! I mean..." I said as I knelt down to pick them up, "Darn? Damn? Crap, how embarrassing."

"Shit is just fine. I've heard worse," he said and laughed as he walked away.

Great, what a day. I see the most gorgeous guy in the world and then promptly make an ass of myself. What's next?

Picking up the dress pants and the hangers, I figured it would be easier to re-hang them in Alterations where I had a large table and could work more comfortably. I looked around for Mr. Sexy as I carried the pants back but no luck, he was gone.

Dropping the pants on the counter, I heard someone in the fitting rooms. *Please let that be Mr. Sexy!* I came around from the counter and almost slammed into Dianna as she stepped out.

"Oh, it's you," I said, disappointed.

"Good to see you too," she snarked. "Expecting someone else?"

"I was hoping you were this guy I just saw."

"Oh great, I didn't think you'd be another Sara."

"No, it's not like that. This guy...I don't know, there was just something about him."

"Where was he?"

"In suits. Checking out the ones that just came in."

"Then give up on him now, he's gay," she deadpanned. "No one ever looks at the new arrivals, and most guys don't care."

"Definitely not gay," I mumbled as I shook my head.

"Well, lots of guys come in and out of here. Obviously, it's the men's department. Maybe he'll be back."

"I hope so."

Chapter Four

Will

The bright store lights of Hargrove's seemed more annoying than usual. I didn't even know why I was there other than needing a change of scenery. The store, with all its people, was the safest place to go. Still, all those people annoyed me and made me wish I had stayed home.

That was until I saw her. With a frustrated look on her face, she straightened up the men's fitting room. As she gathered a stack of dress pants to hang, I moved further into the suit department, not ready to let her out of my sight.

I wondered if she'd be as easy as the others. While I regularly satisfied whatever physical needs I had with the many willing women available to me, this one was different. Most of those eager women were very proud of the work they had done on their bodies, but it left me cold.

A woman should be soft and curvy. The one I watched in the store had a round plump ass and enticingly large breasts that jiggled as she walked. They threatened to spill out of that low cut blouse she wore, and that was something I didn't want to miss. She was quite the delicious package and with her short height, I couldn't help but think of her as 'fun sized', like the candy people gave away on Halloween.

Turning to look at the suits so I wouldn't look like the deviant I really was, I couldn't keep my eyes off her. I looked back at her and our eyes met. *This was going to be easier than I thought. Now to find out her name,* I thought as I smiled and made my way over to her.

***

As I marched towards the exit where my black limo waited at the curb, the crowd parted before me as it always did. Stepping out of the department store's large glass doors, my driver opened the car's back door and waited as I slipped inside.

"Home, sir?" he asked with a slight nod of his bald head.

"You need to ask?" I growled at him.

Stewart had been a driver for my family since I was a child. His appearance was average in every sense of the word, and it gave him the uncanny ability to blend into any crowd. There were many little things that made me suspect he did more for my father years ago than just drive. Stewart started working directly for me fifteen years ago when I took over running the family business.

Stewart and I had a long, complicated history. While we were as close as brothers, there was much about him I didn't know. To call him mysterious was an understatement, yet I trusted him with my life.

As he merged the long black vehicle into traffic, the screen between us lowered. Stewart's brown eyes looked at me through his rear view mirror.

"Meet anyone interesting?" he asked.

"Were you spying on me again?"

"You don't usually take so long."

I noticed he didn't answer my question, but I let it slide. Having known him most of my life, I knew I'd never get an answer.

"I'm a busy man. I shouldn't be wasting time in a department store," I said.

I didn't want to talk about it. I wanted to be alone with my thoughts of her. Deborah, as her name tag so nicely revealed.

Pressing the button, I watched the screen rise between us then took a glance outside to see how far from home we were. Through the tinted glass the city faded into the distance, giving me about thirty minutes alone with my memories.

My mind couldn't help but go back to when I first noticed Deborah piling her arms with hangers. I wasn't paying attention to the hangers though, it was her curves that caught my attention. It wasn't like me to not take what I wanted when I found a woman I desired, but once I got closer, I could tell she was different.

Maybe it was her clothes. They were well made yet obviously her own design. Clothing didn't normally fit a big girl so well. The way her pants hugged her bottom, the soft sheen of the fabric highlighted her curves. Or that blouse...at once showing a little too much cleavage but leaving me wanting so much more.

Unsure if she would recognize me, I avoided her at first by busying myself by the new suits. It annoyed me beyond belief that people knew me while I didn't know them. I valued my privacy, but being the sole heir to the King family fortune made it impossible to find someone who didn't approach me with dollar signs in their eyes. At least it was until today.

Finally giving in to the urge to be closer to her, I approached. What I saw in her sweet brown eyes wasn't recognition though, it was something else. Maybe the same desire I felt for her.

"Sir, will you be heading out tonight?" Stewart's voice came over the speaker system, disturbing my thoughts.

"No, I'll be working tonight. Take the night off."

"Thank you sir, but I have other matters to attend to at the residence. You know I never take the night off. Your security is of utmost importance."

"You don't have to be so formal all the time. You practically raised me," I reminded him.

"Practically and reality are two very different things. You didn't need me, your parents did a fine job before--"

"Just drive," I barked angrily at him. "Every day is enough of a reminder of *before*."

Hearing the speaker quietly shut off, I gazed out the window again. The view changed from tall skyscrapers to low buildings surrounded by grass and trees.

It was the same view as always. None of it different from years ago. A view I hated and looked forward to at the same time. I couldn't help it. I was a creature of habit. Certainly the only reason I still lived where I grew up was more out of habit than anything. Although the home was private. And safe.

I valued those two things above all. Knowing first hand the cost of familiarity, I locked myself away from the public most of the time. Usually a trip into the city would last me quite a while, but this time I was already thinking about returning to Hargrove's.

"Sir? Forgive my intrusion," Stewart said as he rolled down the divider again.

"What is it? And stop with the sir bullshit. You know I can't stand it."

"You know you can call the store for her schedule."

Stewart looked at me through the rear view mirror, his face stoic as always. Reaching for the button, I stopped before clicking to gain my privacy again.

"Thank you, Stewart. It's not every day I get advice on stalking innocent women."

"You are the expert...*sir*," he said. I could tell by the tone of his voice he was reminding me who he thought was really in charge.

The limo jolted forward as Stewart slammed on the brakes. A small red coupe cut us off, forcing us to slow down. Stewart attempted to get around the slow moving car by moving into another lane, but the trucks on either lane beside us wouldn't let us out of our lane.

The trucks picked up speed and blocked us in behind the red car. Stewart turned to look at me, and concern covered his face briefly before changing to an emptiness I had first seen more than twenty-five years ago.

"Will, whatever happens, stay in the car."

"What's going on?" I asked sternly.

He began raising the divider and I hit the button on my side trying to stop it, but it was useless. The limo jerked to the side as one of the trucks careened into us. The other truck moved over, and I realized they were forcing our vehicle wherever they wanted.

Pushing us off the highway, they maneuvered us onto a dirt emergency access road.

The trucks allowed us more space and I wondered why Stewart didn't just slam on his brakes to escape. Turning around, I got my answer.

A silver sedan close behind us had two muscle heads with Aviator sunglasses on. They looked like they meant business. As we drove further down the road with clouds of dust flying everywhere, the two trucks that were alongside the limo veered off, leaving us with only the small red car and their cohorts behind us.

Suddenly, the limo jerked and spun as Stewart slammed on the brakes. Knocked to the side, I scrambled as I heard a quick series of loud pops. The limo stopped, now facing where we came from. As I reached to open the door, a smallish man in a leather motorcycle jacket leapt from the red coupe and rolled on the road before his car burst into flames.

As I ducked from the explosion, I heard the man scream as the fire engulfed him. Stewart left the car. I tried the doors but they wouldn't budge. I was trapped.

The grey sedan's front end was stuck in the rear of our limo. A couple of equally large men exited the back doors of the car with the driver. The man in the passenger seat, now covered in his own blood and glass from the windshield, was obviously dead.

Kicking the door, I tried to get out again. I wanted to help Stewart, who was outnumbered three to one. Meanwhile he glared at the trio, his feet shoulder-width apart, ready for anything.

I had never seen him like this before. The man who dedicated most of his life to raising me was suddenly larger than life with a look of danger in his eyes that would put fear into most men.

In a flash, two of the men launched at him. Stewart fought them off with ease. Wondering where the third man went, I searched for him from the windows of the limo until I spotted him trying to get into the car.

"Bring it asshole, I'm dying to kick your ass," I growled at him.

The doors didn't work for him either. Using the force of his body, he threw himself towards one of the windows. With fists clenched, I waited for him to break into the car. Instead, he bounced off like a toy.

Looking like he grew tired of playing with the two men, Stewart quickly grabbed one by the shoulder in a deadly dance and spun him in one direction as he turned the man's head in the other.

With a sly grin, he beckoned the other man closer, who paused, seeing the fate of his comrade.

A flash of light sparked out of the corner of my eye and a loud bang hit the window next to me. I turned to see the third man holding a gun towards the car, but again nothing happened. As fast as lightning, Stewart pulled out a sleek black gun. He fired one shot at my assailant, then kicked the man attacking him in the temple, causing both men to drop to the ground.

Stewart spat at the ground, looking confident and deadly as he surveyed the three men and then walked over to the limo. The car door opened for him with ease. Without a word, he smoothed his hand over his head pushing his nonexistent hair back and put his driver's cap back on. As he began driving, he suddenly became my peaceful, aging driver again, only now with a satisfied smirk on his face.

This wasn't the first time I had been in danger, and I knew it wouldn't be the last. Each time they attacked they got a little closer, but the end result was always the same--they never got what they came for.

The car slowed at the large, ornate iron gates of King Manor. No matter how many years it had been since I rode in the car with my mother, the gates always reminded me of her. She would tell stories about a trip to the French countryside she and my father took before I was born. Originally, these gates were part of an ancient abandoned monastery, and she fell in love with them. She told her stories with such vivid detail I easily imagined the gates outside an old dilapidated abbey instead of blocking access to the King family's mansion.

While I traveled extensively for business, I never took time for personal trips. They were too dangerous, so I never saw the monastery myself. Filling most of my days with work, I made sure I didn't have time for social events. I didn't want any part of them. My father enjoyed the spotlight, and it killed him. I had no interest in being a person people felt familiar with.

As the limo went through the gate, I pulled my phone out of my pocket. Stewart had a point. It was easy enough to get the information I wanted.

"Thank you for calling Hargrove's," the automated voice on the other end of the call answered. "You've reached the Human Resources department. Your call will be answered shortly."

"Human Resources, this is Joan."

"Joan, this is William King. I need you to give me some employee information." I said.

"On a specific employee? I'm sorry, Mr. King, but I can't do that," she said, her voice shaking.

"It's her schedule. You can and you will do it. Her name is Deborah and she's in Men's."

"Yes--yes, Mr. King, one moment. I found her. Deborah Hansen. It looks like she's a new tailor in the men's department. I only have this week's schedule, but it looks like she works days. Would you like me to--"

"That's enough, Joan. Thank you," I said as I hung up.

Stewart pulled the car up to the stone steps of the large gothic mansion I called my home. Stepping out of the car, the doors now working for me too, I glimpsed the large fountain at the center of the circular driveway, another one of my mother's finds.

Crossing behind the car, I ignored the damage, knowing the car would be replaced. The oval fountain, with its three jets of water quietly shooting up into the air, caused cascading streams. Pulling a coin out of my pocket, I tossed it into the fountain as my mother taught me to do as a child.

It was a habit I was unable to break, no matter how much it tugged at my heart. In all these years, the only thing missing from the ritual she taught me was the wish. The wishes stopped when I was eight.

Turning back to the building, I wondered if it always looked so cold. The grey stone of the exterior made the peaks of the turrets look sharper as it stood before the bright sun in the sky.

Living in the mansion my entire life, it surprised me when I noticed things like that. Stewart and I were the home's only residents, unless one counted the small team of people who maintained the property.

A long time ago, the mansion was home to parties and gatherings, but I stopped all of that. I didn't need people kissing my ass because they wanted to get into my wallet. I certainly wasn't going to entertain them for fun. Most women jumped at the chance to visit King Manor and spend the night in my bed. I didn't need the ruse of a party to get them here.

Entering the large hall, the sound of my shoes echoed down the long corridors. I walked straight to the back of the house to my study, my favorite place to relax. It was my hideaway and the only part of the house I changed from when my parents lived there.

Lining two adjacent walls were built-in bookcases with my vast collection of both fiction and non-fiction. They were my pleasure in life. I often found myself enjoying the company of characters in a book more than the people I had to associate with in real life.

Along the next wall was a long contemporary bar made of a black and brown granite and wood. As I walked to the bar to pour myself two fingers of scotch, I unbuttoned and removed my suit jacket then tossed it onto the sleek black leather desk chair in the middle of the room next to my desk.

The back wall of the study was made entirely of glass and faced the valley. The sloping hills were dotted with deep green trees and dried vegetation from the recent drought. The quiet view was comforting to me, and I often sat on the flagstone patio for some fresh air as I gathered my thoughts.

Picking up the book I was reading from a glass side table, I went outside with my drink and thought about Deborah Hansen. I loved how her black hair framed her pretty full face, hitting just below her jaw line. Or how her smile made me think the world was a better place just because she was in it.

I tried pushing her out of my mind, but it was useless. Not only did I find her beautiful, but I could tell she was smart and funny, too. It was a dangerous combination for a woman as far as I was concerned. And it was one I was unable to resist.

Reaching for the laptop I kept on the patio, I checked my schedule for the next day. After sending a quick email, I changed a meeting so I would have the morning free. I knew Deborah was working tomorrow and I hoped the store would be empty.

It felt like such a struggle. I normally preferred my quiet, lonely existence. That was the only reason I left her without getting to know more. I desperately wanted to be alone, to continue my private, safe, secluded existence, but I needed to get to know the short, curvy tailor even more.

Chapter Five

Deborah

As I arrived at work the next morning, I vowed that no matter who was there, I was going to make sure I was either in tailoring or in suits. Mr. Sexy had to come back and I needed to make sure I wouldn't miss him.

Entering the men's department, my black Mary Jane pumps clicked against the marble floor. I wore my favorite wine colored v-neck silk blouse with a black circle skirt I was convinced made my hips look smaller.

"I see you're dressed for Mr. Sexy today," Dianna took a step back and looked me up and down as she fanned herself with her hand.

"Thanks," I said, laughing. "I'm going to be in suits today if that's okay."

"Sure, but you might have to fight Sara for it."

With an exaggerated look, Dianna turned her eyes towards suits, and I followed her gaze. Prepping the register for the day stood a tall, beautiful woman with hair the color of honey. She looked to be in her early twenties with her sun-bleached highlights and athletic build. A lace cami peeked out of her snug suit jacket. It was obvious from her jiggling she didn't bother to wear a bra.

Give her a chance, don't hate her yet, I thought. As she stepped out from behind the register, my eyes flew to her long and lean legs sticking out from her too-short skirt.

"You've got to be kidding me," I muttered.

"Just wait until you see her in action," Dianna said.

"Can't you do anything about it? You're the manager."

"She's our highest earner. They don't care what she wears or how much she flirts, she's making the store a lot of money."

I sighed and reminded myself that maybe she wasn't so bad. Maybe despite her leaving the department a mess and dressing like a slut, she was nice.

"Yeah, because that's how the world works," I muttered sarcastically to myself.

"Oh, it looks like she's already found her first victim," Dianna said as she walked away.

I looked back towards suits and couldn't believe my eyes. There was Mr. Sexy in the flesh! Well in a suit, but underneath... *Get a grip, Deborah!*

My eyes caressed his broad shoulders down the taper of his back until they stopped at a small hand on his bicep. *Oh, hell no!* As I quickly made my way over, my shoes clicking 'that bitch' with each step, I could hear Sara's soft voice and it made me even angrier.

"No, I'm sure there isn't a Deborah Hansen here. But I can help you with whatever you want," she purred.

"Don't touch me," Mr. Sexy growled.

Even though I couldn't see his face, I could tell by how quickly she stepped back that he meant it.

"The tailor from yesterday. Get. Her. Now," he said, as if he thought she didn't understand him.

In shock to hear that he was looking for me, I couldn't speak. Quickly replaying yesterday in my head, I wondered if I did something to make him so stern. Coming up from behind him, I softly reached up and touched Mr. Sexy on his back between his shoulder blades. He turned, his eyes narrowed and his face stern until he recognized me and flashed a smile.

"Just who I've been looking for," he said while his eyes never left mine.

Sara walked away looking briefly defeated and annoyed until another male customer entered the department. She pounced on him like a lion after a gazelle. Happy Sara found someone to busy herself with, I focused my attention on Mr. Sexy.

"You were looking for me?" I asked.

"Yes. I need a new suit and after seeing you handle them yesterday, I knew you were the girl for me."

He winked as he finished speaking and I grinned back, embarrassed that he brought up my dropping the pants. Was he teasing or flirting? I needed to get a grip, he was probably just being nice.

"Sure, right this way," I finally replied, my voice shaking.

Leading him to the suits, my legs felt like jelly. I couldn't believe this man made me so nervous. As I took a deep breath, I narrowed my eyes on the racks and convinced myself he was anyone other than Mr. Sexy.

"Is there anything in particular you're looking for?"

"How about this one?" he asked as he pulled out my favorite--a two-button navy Tom Ford suit with light blue pin-striping. I admired the tailoring of Tom Ford's suits, he definitely knew how to dress a man to look sexy, strong, and elegant at the same time.

"I can tell you that you'd look great in it," I said, immediately stunned by the words that flew out of my mouth.

"I think I'd look better with you beside me."

My heart did flips in my chest and I paused to catch my breath. I couldn't believe it! *He was flirting with me!* I carried the suit as we headed towards the fitting area and felt his fingers briefly touch the small of my back, sending a heat throughout my body that I hadn't felt in a long time.

As I waited for him to change into the suit, I quickly gave myself the once over in the mirror. Pinching my cheeks, I wished I wasn't so pale, but there was nothing I could do about that now. Using a couple of bobby pins, I took the front of my hair and twisted it around into a quick side braid and pinned it away from my face. I needed to get precise measurements for his suit, and I didn't need my hair falling in my face as I did it.

Stepping out of the dressing room, Mr. Sexy already looked perfect. That suit was made for him. His shoulders filled the jacket, making a perfect line across his back. I could already see I'd have to let out the sleeves a little for his large biceps. As I evaluated the suit from a distance, he spotted me. I quickly bit my lip to stop myself from saying anything stupid, and I motioned for him to join me at the three-way mirror.

I pulled up a small step stool to check and adjust the shoulders. Smoothing the material over his back, I slowed my hands down, enjoying the feel of his body underneath and imagining what it looked and felt like without his clothing.

Accidentally letting out a long, lust-filled sigh, I looked up at the mirror and saw Mr. Sexy looking back at me. His eyes looked more green than hazel in this light. As I met his gaze, I suddenly felt insecure, like he was undressing me with his eyes, not the other way around. Heat spread over my face and embarrassed, I looked away and stepped back. Forgetting I was on the stool, I stumbled and reached out to him to keep from falling.

"Didn't realize tailoring was such a dangerous position," he said.

"Oh, you wouldn't believe the dangerous positions I can get myself into."

His laughter was throaty and deep, which made me want him more. My pulse beat loudly in my ears as I marked the sleeves, making my way in front of him. Slipping my hand into the front of the buttoned jacket to make sure the jacket had enough space when buttoned, I felt the heat of his body through the dress shirt.

I didn't know what was going on with me, but Mr. Sexy made me want to do things that were far from professional. Opening my hand, I slid my palm over his snugly buttoned shirt, hoping he wouldn't notice.

"Deborah," he said. I jerked my hand away. "It might be easier if you unbuttoned the jacket."

Nodding, stunned over what was happening, I unbuttoned the single thick plastic button he used to close the jacket. I breathed him in deeply. His scent made me think of an herb garden, fresh and clean but with a hint of spice. Before I could muster my courage again, he took my hand and placed it on his chest.

Ignoring his intense gaze, my hand traveled up the smooth fabric of his shirt and towards his shoulder. The heat of his skin came through the material and as my hand slid down over the flexed muscle of his pecs, it was even easier to imagine him without the shirt. Moving my hand down further, I explored the hard terrain of his abs until Sara's high-pitched giggle brought me back to reality.

The last thing I wanted was for someone to catch me feeling up a customer. Even if I was pretty sure no one would blame me once they saw Mr. Sexy.

"I--I'm sorry about that," I stammered as I looked away and stepped back from him.

"Don't be, I enjoyed it," he said with that same crooked smile he gave me the day before.

Out of nervous habit, I reached up to push my hair out of my eyes, but found it still secured in place. It was official, while he was Mr. Sexy, I was Miss Idiot. I really needed to get a hold of myself. Normally I kept my cool around gorgeous men. Was I that out of practice?

"I'll take care of your inseam now."

"Deborah..." He breathed my name, and I gulped at the air as my heart beat even faster.

I looked up into his eyes again, the flecks of green flashing in the store lights. My throat felt dry, like every ounce of fluid now came out of the palms of my hands, which trembled by my sides. I really needed to get a grip of myself and calm down.

"Yes?" I said, once again using the only word I could say.

"Why did you change your hair? It was already beautiful before."

Closing the distance between us, he gently began sliding the bobby pins from my hair, loosening my braid. As my hair fell and brushed my cheek, I breathed in his scent again and enjoyed the heat coming off his body. I couldn't tear my eyes away from his if my life depended on it. Entranced, I didn't even realize his lips drew closer to mine.

His soft yet firm lips made my head swim. I parted my lips, waiting for more, wanting more, when the gentle ding of the overhead speaker sounded.

"Oh!" I stepped back from him, suddenly aware of where we were as my legs felt like jelly. Heat creeped across my cheeks again as he gave me that knowing grin. "Your inseam. I have to measure your inseam," I whispered. *Shit! What's wrong with me?*

"Say my name," he commanded.

My brow wrinkled. There was no way I was going to call him Mr. Sexy to his face. He must have meant his real name, and I'd remember if he gave it to me.

"Mr..." *Sexy*, I thought. "I don't think you told me what your name is."

"You really don't recognize me?" he asked with a raised brow.

"Should I?"

A hearty laugh escaped his throat and his eyes seemed to soften even more. "No, it's actually a relief. I'm pretty well known in Canyon Cove. Wealthy businessman and all that."

I shrugged. I really could care less. Mr. Sexy would still be Mr. Sexy even if he didn't have two nickels to rub together. Besides, he was in Hargrove's buying an expensive suit. What else could he be besides a wealthy businessman?

"I guess I don't keep on top of that kind of stuff. It's never really interested me," I said as I pinned my hair back again and grabbed my measuring tape.

"It's Will."

"What will?" I asked as I knelt in front of him, trying to get my mind back on my job.

"My name," he said then laughed. "It's Will. Call me Will."

Embarrassed, I only nodded. I couldn't believe how much of an effect this man, Mr. Sexy Will, was having over me. Happy to not be standing on my jelly legs anymore, I slowly brought the tape up his inseam to his crotch.

The pants had a flat front and were a touch too tight, enough that I could see the outline of his...w*ait, that's an erection!* Doug had been the last man I had been with over two years ago, but I knew a hard-on when I saw it. Was Will teasing me?

Slowly letting my eyes travel up his body, they met with his. The playful twinkle in his eye combined with his knowing smile was enough to tell me he meant for me to see it.

I didn't say anything, just made notes of the length of the pants and marked the cuffs where they needed to be hemmed. But I couldn't stop thinking about it. It was right there! And my eyes kept moving back up to the front of his pants.

Thinking about how he let me touch his chest and later kissed me, I realized I might never get a second chance at this. My pulse beat loudly, rhythmically. *No regrets, no regrets.* Pulling the measuring tape out again, I brought it up his inseam, but then slowly moved my hand over the bulge in his pants like it was the most normal thing to do.

"Does that need to be measured, too?" he asked playfully.

"Yes, as a matter of fact, it does," I said, glad to finally feel like my old self again. "It's the latest innovation in tailoring. You can read about it in GQ." *Or more likely Dear Penthouse,* I thought, forcing myself to keep a straight face.

I looked up at him, my eyes wide and innocent as I tried to act like I believed every word I told him as my hand traveled the length of his manhood, surprised by its size.

"I believe I read about that." He winked as he grinned at me. "But I think you're doing it wrong, I believe the tailor is supposed to be more hands on. You know, for a proper fit."

The playfulness from before suddenly became mischievous. Without missing a beat, Will unbuttoned his slacks and unzipped as I sat back on my heels, waiting to see how far this would go and excited to see it through. I couldn't wait to see how daring my Mr. Sexy was.

I caught a glimpse of light grey cotton boxer briefs. Then his hand reached under the waistband. I held my breath in anticipation.

"Deborah!" Sara called from the cash register. "Did you take the measuring tape? I always keep one here for emergencies."

I turned towards her voice, annoyed even more at her presence but hoping she wouldn't come back into the fitting area.

"Never mind! I found it," she yelled before I could answer her.

"Now where were we?" I said as I turned back to Will, but he was gone. "Dammit! Where'd he go?"

I ran into the dressing rooms, but they were empty. Entering the suit department, I looked for his tall figure but saw nothing except Sara.

"Hey Sara, did you see that customer from earlier? The one who asked for me?"

"Oh, you mean the one you stole from me? No, not since you whisked him away. Why?"

"No reason. Just asking."

I wasn't about to tell her what happened. Quickly making my way through the department, I kept an eye out for his dark hair and muscular body but didn't see anything. I could have called security since he was wearing a very expensive suit, but I didn't want him to come back because he had to. I wanted him to come back because he wanted to, like he did earlier. I'd just have to wait for that happen again. If it happened again.

Chapter Six

Deborah

A week had passed since Mr. Sexy left me anxious to see his unwrapped package. I'd be lying if I didn't say I fantasized about what might have happened next if there was no one in the store at all except for the two of us. Each day dragged by as I waited for him to return, my measuring tape close at hand.

"Why so glum?" Dianna asked as I arrived at work that morning.

"Just missing Mr. Sexy."

"He's still a no-show?"

"Yeah, not since he tried on that suit," I said, intentionally leaving out anything else that happened between us. "I doubt he'll be back. It's such a shame too, he was so hot!"

She giggled, then patted my back as she gave me a mock-sympathetic look. "Well, at least you'll be busy. Today's your interview for the design contest, right?"

"Yes, at 11. Do I look okay? They'll be judging what I'm wearing as much as my portfolio."

"Relax, you always look great."

Knowing it was an important day, I wore one of my favorite designs--a long plum silk jersey halter dress with a keyhole opening to show off my cleavage. I designed the dress so whoever wore it could show as little or as much as they wanted without the keyhole being obvious when closed.

Below the keyhole, I hand-ruched a thick waistband, which gave me the appearance of an hourglass silhouette. That was one of the nice things about designing my own clothes - nothing ever fit me right in stores. I was always too short, too round, too everything. So making my own designs gave me the ability to custom fit clothes to my body.

As I waited for my interview time to arrive, I noticed every man who walked past the suit department. Sometimes my breath would catch when I saw a man I thought was Will, but it never was.

Maybe I took things too far. I began to scold myself for acting so slutty, but I really didn't regret it. Those minutes with my Mr. Sexy was the most exciting thing to happen to me in a long time.

Riding the elevator to the corporate floor, I resigned myself to giving up. He had no reason to come back to the store, there were plenty of other high end department stores with chubby girls he could flirt with. For all I knew, it was just a game. It meant nothing and he was just pushing to see how far I would take it.

But he came back for me. That had to mean something. I needed to stop thinking about it. I wasn't doing myself any favors. Men as handsome and sexy as Will didn't want a girl like me. He was probably laughing at me just like Doug did a few weeks ago in his car.

The elevator doors opened, and I stepped out onto the white marble floor and followed it down the hall to a large archway, under which was a walnut desk with a pretty young African American girl chewing gum.

She looked up at me and flashed a perfect smile. "Hi, are you Deborah Hanson? They're waiting for you," she said as she motioned to the glass door behind her.

"Waiting? I was told 11. I'm early."

She leaned forward and the light hit her hair, revealing it to be a deep purple shade. I got a strong whiff of the pink bubble gum in her mouth as she whispered.

"Apparently the last girl here was just wasting their time." She used air quotes as she finished her sentence then sat back, satisfied she shared her piece of gossip. "Go ahead through those doors. Good luck!"

"Thanks," I mumbled as I walked past her desk with my tablet and through the oversized glass doors to a small conference room.

With my shoulders back and my head held high, I looked at the three people seated at a long table at the end of the room. I recognized the Women's Fashions buyer from her photo in the hall. A woman in her fifties with larger than life bright red hair and small delicate features, Amanda Cunning was known to be very particular about the new designers she introduced to the store.

I paused in my trek to the blue conference chair set up across the table from them when I recognized the older man seated next to Amanda. It was renowned fashion designer Tim Ross. Tim Ross's designs were classy yet fashion forward at the same time, a feat many designers tried to accomplish but failed. He was one of main reasons I wanted to become a designer. The highlight of my collection was an evening gown that gave a nod to his influence. I couldn't wait to show him.

Last was a small, thin woman with her black hair pulled back into such a tight bun. I wondered if her face would collapse if she loosened it. Wearing a very traditional navy business suit, I assumed she was one of Hargrove's higher ups. Maybe even Mrs. Hargrove. I knew nothing of the Hargrove family except that they created the fine department store decades ago.

Smiling as I approached them, I extended my hand while holding on to my tablet with the other.

"Hi, I'm Deborah Hansen. Thank you for allowing me into the contest, I know it was last minute."

"Well, we didn't really have much choice now, did we? I'm Claudine Calvin," said the woman with the tight bun, "Director of Acquisitions. I believe this has been the worse turnout for this contest in years. Kylie at the desk out there likes to talk, I'm sure she told you what happened to the last contestant."

I smiled, not wanting to answer and get Kylie in trouble.

"Yes, the turnout has been surprising, Claudine," Amanda said. "So when Human Resources called to submit your name and said you were a friend of Joshua Cane's, let's just say I was hopeful."

"Is that why Hargrove's hasn't had a collection in Fashion Week for the last three years?" Tim asked.

"Precisely. I wasn't going to have one of my designers create a collection and then dash their hopes of going if we had an amazing winner. And I refuse to show more than one collection at Fashion Week," Amanda said. "I believe you should show one fabulous collection and leave them wanting more. Now Miss Hansen, will your designs interest us or leave us cold?"

"My collection is perfect for Hargrove's," I said, stepping forward and resting my tablet in front of Tim where they could all see it. "Even though it's a mixture of day and evening looks, the overall cohesiveness works. I chose colors inspired by nature and styles that are flattering to all body types."

Swiping the screen slowly, I showed them each of the pieces I created and how some of them could mix and match with others. While I assumed Amanda and Claudine would make the decision, my focus was on Tim Ross, who nodded and smiled as he looked at my sketches. At the end, I let the tablet do a slideshow of the images to give the impression of them walking down a runway.

"Very impressive, Miss Hansen," Tim said, and I fought the urge to jump up and hug him. "I especially enjoyed that show-stopping gown at the end. Did you also design the dress you're wearing?"

"Oh, you have no idea how much that means to me, Mr. Ross. Your designs have been so inspirational. I did design that gown with you in mind and yes, this dress is mine, too."

"Beautiful work. I can see you have an eye for detail."

"Can you get us samples by next month?" Amanda asked.

"Samples?" My head spun. Samples meant I needed to buy fabric and create each of the pieces. The cutting and sewing wasn't the hard part, I could create samples fairly quick. They didn't need to be fit-on-model perfect, but they did need to be well constructed. The problem was I didn't have money for fabric. I'd have to figure something out. "No problem. I can get you samples by then," I said confidently.

"Perfect," Amanda said. "We have several other contestants to meet with this week, but based on what we've seen so far, I'm pretty sure we've found our winner." She turned to look at Tim and Claudine, and they both nodded. "Kylie will be in touch with you to schedule the sample viewing."

"Thank you! Oh, thank you so much!" I was so excited I ran to the other side of the table and hugged each of them before picking up my tablet and exiting the room before they could change their minds.

"Sounds like they liked you," Kylie said as I left the conference room.

"I knew they'd love my designs. Now I just need to make the samples. Guess I'll see you in a month!"

Stepping out of the elevator, I floated on air as I walked back to my department. I purposefully walked past each of the women's departments and imagined my designs on the mannequins. It would be a dream come true to see my collection in the store, but there was one big hurdle--money.

If I worked extra hours, I could borrow from my rent money now and be able to pay rent with my next paycheck. I'd have to make sure with Dianna that there were extra hours available, but I was positive she'd figure out a way for me to get them. I knew the days would be long and I'd have to work on the samples late at night, but a little less sleep never hurt anybody.

"You look happy." The deep voice of Mr. Sexy coming from behind me startled and excited me at the same time.

I spun around to face him. Looking gorgeous as always, this time he was in a classic three-piece brown suit with tan pin-striping. Still on my high from the interview, I hugged him. I probably would have kissed him if he wasn't so damn tall.

"The most amazing thing happened! They want to see samples of my collection!"

I spoke too fast because I was so excited, but he didn't seem to mind. He just smiled and looked happy for me.

"I've been looking for you," he said.

"Well, you found me." I wanted to say *it's about time* but didn't want to lose him because of my snark. *Best to let him get to know me and then he can realize I'm a wise-ass.*

"I'll pick you up tonight at 6pm," he said then turned to go.

"Wait, what?" I asked, confused.

"We're going on a date. I'll pick you up at six."

"No, I can't."

I couldn't believe the words that came out of my mouth. How could I say no to a date with Mr. Sexy? It's not even like it was a question. He expected me to just go with him...and I didn't have a problem with that.

"What do you mean no?" he asked, obviously not used to hearing the word.

"I need to work. I need some extra hours so I can cover the rent money I'm taking to make samples."

"I'll give you the money. See you at six."

He began walking away while I shook my head. "No!" I called out to him. He turned back and looked at me, confused. "I'm not going to take your money, Will."

"Fine, but I'll still be here at six."

I stood there dumbfounded as he walked away, cutting his way through the crowd as they parted before him.

"Was that him? The elusive Mr. Sexy?" Dianna asked as she approached.

"Yup. That was him," I said numbly.

"Hmm, he looks familiar. Maybe it's just the suit. What's wrong? You don't sound happy."

"I am happy. Today's been one of the best days of my life. He's taking me out on a date."

"So what's the problem?"

"I was going to work late. I need some extra money. I'm a finalist in the competition and I need to have samples ready for next month."

"Awesome! Go out tonight and celebrate with Mr. Sexy. You can worry about real life tomorrow."

Chapter Seven

Will

"Stewart, I am going on a date. Do you realize how ridiculous I'll look showing up with you?"

In my large, sparsely furnished bedroom, I paced the dark marble floor, annoyed to have this conversation about my date.

"Will, *sir*," he said sarcastically. Stewart never liked when I disagreed with him. "No woman is going to turn down a limo ride. If she knows who you are, then I'm sure she's expecting it."

"This girl is different. But no, she doesn't know who I am. Not exactly at least."

"Don't you think she should know?"

"It's not important. I'll tell her when I'm ready."

"But sir--"

"Mind your place, Stewart!" I growled at him.

"My place in this matter isn't as your driver and head of security but as your friend."

I didn't say anything. What could I say? Stewart was my confidant and had been there for me my entire life.

"Fine, you're right. Maybe she needs to know, but not just yet. Please, let me just enjoy this date."

"Did you do what I asked?"

"I know you're trying to protect me, Stewart. Eventually you need to realize I need to have a life. I'm tired of being alone and I haven't been able to get her out of my mind since I met her. If someone is going to kidnap or attack me while I'm out, then maybe it's just meant to be. You can't protect me from everything."

"You don't know what you're saying. I've dedicated my life to protecting you from harm. There are people out there you could never begin to understand."

"I'm done discussing this. I am taking Deborah out on a date. This is the first woman I've ever wanted to know more than just physically. Will you back off?"

"Answer my question. As head of your security, did you do as I asked?"

"Yes, but not because you asked. It was the only way I could get the table I wanted on such short notice."

"And driving?"

"If it will get you off my back, then drive. It'll give Deborah and I a chance to get to know each other better anyway."

Chapter Eight

Deborah

At 6pm on the dot, I made my way to the time clocks to check out of work. The employee only area was on the second floor, in the back of the store. After being in the bright lights and glistening floors of the sales floor, the employee area looked drab and dirty by comparison.

A dark, rust colored rug lined the long corridor to the twin time clocks. As I approached them, I saw an envelope taped to one and guessed it was out of order. I was wrong.

With neatly printed letters, the cover of the envelope had my name on it. I quickly looked around, but as usual there was nobody near the time clocks but me. Pulling out the off-white card inside, my heart raced in anticipation.

Deborah,
Please meet me at the main entrance.
Will

How did he get back here? I slowly realized he didn't need to come back here at all. Just because the card was from him didn't mean he even wrote it. I knew how rich people worked, they always hired someone else to do their dirty work.

Geez, get a grip on yourself. I had to admit I was a little more than offended that he offered me money. Who did he think he was? Did he have to get his own way that much that he was willing to pay for it?

I sighed as I headed towards the main entrance. As usual, I was overreacting. He was only trying to be nice. I just wish he chose a different way of going about it.

Easily spotting him standing in the crowd of people moving in and out of the store, all my annoyance melted away. Dressed in that chocolate brown three-piece suit with the buttoned vest peeking out from the jacket, he looked good enough to eat. Something about the suit made me think of couples going out to a speakeasy and sneaking some alcohol, but it suited him perfectly.

Will had the same cold expression on his face as he did when Sara tried to help him. I began wondering if it was his normal expression and if the smiling, flirting man I was getting to know was something only I saw.

"Hi, I hope you weren't waiting long."

"Let's go," he grumbled as he took me by my elbow and guided me towards the door. "I hate crowds."

"Sorry, it's the time. There's always an after-work rush."

He steered me through the double glass doors of Hargrove's and outside, where a long black limo waited at the curb. An athletic man in a black suit and driver's cap opened the back door and waited.

"Is that for us?"

Will grunted. The driver nodded at him as Will took my hand and helped me get into the car. I slid over as far as I could on the long black leather seat that made up the rear of the limo. Along one side of the limo was another long couch, while across from that was a small bar. I had never been in a limo before in my life. I wasn't sure if I should be impressed or not.

"Is this how you always travel?"

"Unfortunately, yes."

"Why do it if you don't like it?"

Looking at me, he sighed as he thought about the question. His face softened slightly before returning to stone cold.

"It's complicated and not something I care to discuss."

As the car began moving, Mr. Sexy grew quieter. I didn't know what to say, but I had to say something. The silence was unbearable and I'd be damned if my date with him was going to be a bust.

Gazing out the window, I looked for something to talk about. I recognized the canyon road leading out of the city to the beach. The colors of the canyon and the sky inspired my collection, and I couldn't stop thinking about the samples I needed to create. As we entered the quaint beach area of Canyon Cove, I recognized a street name.

"Oh, there's Laguna Way. I should've known it would be down here," I accidentally said out loud.

"What's on Laguna?"

"A fabric shop I've heard about called Make It Work. They have a lot of fabrics and trim you can't find anywhere else in the United States. I've always wanted to go there."

He leaned forward and hit a switch in the ceiling. The divider between us and the driver lowered.

"Stewart, can you turn around? There's a fabric shop back there Deborah would like to go to."

"Oh no, really. We don't have to go," I said. "I don't have the money to buy anything anyway."

"We're on a date, Deborah. Call me old fashioned, but a woman doesn't pay when she's asked on a date. Let's go look at the fabrics. I should've brought flowers for our date, let this be how you let me make that up to you."

I stared at him in shock. This wasn't much different than him offering me money earlier for the fabrics, but at the same time it was. I didn't know if it was the leather of the seats that did it, or the simple fact that I knew we all needed help sometimes, but I nodded and gave the driver the address.

"You have no idea what this means to me. You know I need fabric to make my samples. I honestly don't have the money though. This is really just the most amazing thing anyone has offered to do. I promise when I can I will pay you back."

"Nonsense, you don't pay back gifts."

"Sir," Stewart said as he pulled up in front of the simple white clapboard building that housed the store, "please stay in the car. I'm running in to do a quick sweep of the building."

Will sighed and looked out the window as his driver's words hung in the air. I didn't know why there was such a huge concern over security. Canyon Cove had very affluent sections with plenty of wealthy people, even billionaires, but I never heard of any crimes against them.

"I can go in alone. I don't mind. And--" I said until I got interrupted.

"No!" Will interrupted me with a growl. "Stewart, Miss Hansen and I are going into the store."

He opened the door and got out in a huff. I expected Stewart to argue, but instead he looked forward and raised the divider. Will held his hand out and helped me out of the car, not letting go of it as we started walking into the store.

As with most shops on Canyon Cove's coast, the building exteriors were older and plain. Above the door was a blue sign with the shop's name in a stylized handwritten lettering. A chime played as we entered the door.

"Welcome to Make It Work," said a heavyset man with a shaved head and several piercings. He was in the center of a large combination check out and fabric cutting area. He was flipping through the latest issue of Vogue and didn't bother to look up from the magazine.

Behind him, aisles of fabrics dominated the store from floor to ceiling. Broken down by type of fabric, it would've been easy for me to find what I needed for the samples, but I wanted to look at everything. With my unreliable car, the coast was too far for me to drive. I didn't know if I'd ever get back here.

"You're sure you're okay with this? I know what I'm looking for, but I really wanted to look around, too."

Will nodded. "The restaurant can wait," he said. "I know how important this is to you."

I could have stayed in that store forever, but I wasn't about to waste my first date with Mr. Sexy shopping for fabric. Like Dianna said, tonight was about my date, real life could wait until tomorrow.

I managed to get the fabrics I needed for my samples. My favorite was an ocean blue delicate chiffon with a faded white print that resembled wave crests for the gown. The chiffon was so light and soft I knew it would flow beautifully.

Other fabrics I got were a black-brown textured brocade that was perfect for a jacket, a silk-wool with abstract purple watercolor flowers with pale green stems that would make a breathtaking skirt, and silk jersey in several colors because I loved how easy it was to drape.

The limo was still parked at the curb when Will and I left Make It Work. Stewart didn't open the door for us or say a word the rest of the night.

"It shouldn't be a far drive to The Breezes from here," Will said.

"The Breezes? Is that where we're going?"

"Yes, it's the best place to watch the sun set into the ocean. Plus their food is pretty good. Have you ever been there?"

"No. I don't think I even know anyone who has. Am I dressed okay? I would've changed clothes if I knew we were going to such a fancy place."

"You look stunning. Trust me, you're perfect just the way you are."

"Won't I stand out? I'm sure the other women there will be really dressed up, or maybe more conservative."

"There won't be other women there. There won't be anyone else there. I value my privacy above all other things. I bought the restaurant for the night."

"Seriously?"

Instead of answering, Will motioned for me to look out the window. We were pulling up the steep circular driveway of The Breezes, and there were no other cars around. Known almost more for the line of cars that extended around the block than for it being the most prestigious restaurant in all of Canyon Cove, The Breezes had a waiting list that some said was close to a year long.

The restaurant sat on the top of a cliff along the shoreline. It was a Spanish style, white stone one-story building with gardens of lush tropical flowers and trees surrounding it. When our car stopped at the main entrance, an attendant stepped forward and opened the door to the limo.

"Good evening, Mr. King," he said as we stepped onto the walkway in front of the building.

"One day we'll get here earlier and I'll show you the gardens," Will said.

"So you've been here before?" I asked as we entered the restaurant, our voices echoing against the Spanish ceramic tile floor.

"Yes, but never like this."

"I bet you say that to all the girls," I teased.

"No, I don't," he said, his face serious. "I know we don't know each other well, but you're different than the others."

"Why? Because I'm fat?"

Anger covered his face, and I immediately regretted saying those words. He didn't need to hear about my insecurities. Under the stress from the contest and being so broke, my mouth proved it had a mind of its own.

"What do you think this is? Charity?" His voice boomed throughout the empty restaurant. "I bought the restaurant for the night because the table I wanted was booked and because I'd rather be alone with you than surrounded by a bunch of strangers."

Grabbing my arm a little roughly, he led me into a small dining room with blue mosaic tile surrounding a fireplace. Directly in front of me was a large glass window framed by palm trees with a table set for two. I stepped up to the window and looked out at the amber sun slowly sinking into the ocean, with the sandy white beach below. At this height, I could see the shoreline for miles.

Standing there quietly, I watched the waves crash on the beach, their white crests reminding me of the fabric Will just bought me for my samples.

"I'm sorry," I whispered. "I don't know what's wrong with me."

"I'll show you what's wrong with you," he said.

He walked into the next room, and I followed without thinking.

"Why is it so dark in here?"

In front of me was a similar window to the one in the room with the view, except this one was dark.

"This window faces the other side, with the gardens," he said and flicked the light switch.

With the lights turned on, the window became a mirror. And I was facing it. I quickly turned away.

"No. Look at yourself," he said as he stepped closer to me, moving behind me. "Really look at yourself. See what I see."

With a habit of avoiding full-length mirrors like the plague, I hadn't really looked at myself in years. My black bob had grown out a bit and was just past my chin. I had opened the peek-a-boo keyhole to show off more of my assets before meeting Will.

The dress looked even better than I could have imagined. The gathering around the waist made me even more hourglass than I planned. I knew the dress looked good on me, but I never stopped to realize I looked good, too. It wasn't just the smoke and mirrors of the dress.

"A few weeks ago, I was in the suit department at Hargrove's," he said, his voice low and husky. "I turned around when I heard the shuffling of another person and spotted an angel. She had black hair, the perfect juxtaposition against her creamy skin, and it drew me to her. But as I approached, I realized she wasn't an angel at all."

His strong hands felt warm on my bare shoulders. Dropping his head down, he pressed his cheek against my hair and slowly inhaled, sending chills up my spine. Frozen with desire for him, I waited for what might happen next.

"No angel could get away with flaunting so much cleavage, let alone ignite the bad thoughts of what I want to do there," he said as his fingers lightly traced the exposed skin in the opening of my dress.

"Deborah," he whispered in my ear, "you are incredibly sexy. I won't lie, I've been with many women, but I've never wanted one as badly as I want you. Your hair, your face, your personality, and your body. Everything is perfect."

Feeling his large hands slip down the sides of the thin fabric of my dress, I felt naked before him. My breath caught as my body reacted to his touch, wanting more.

"Excuse me, Mr. King," a woman's voice spoke softly behind us. "Dinner is served."

Will let out a sigh before straightening to his full height. "Thank you, we'll be right there."

Turning to face him, I looked up into his hazel eyes to find them a dark green. Reaching up, I grabbed his brown striped tie and pulled him down to kiss him.

The moment our lips touched, my body ached for more. I pressed myself against him as his fingers wound into my hair and pulled my head back. His mouth left mine and moved slowly down my neck, stopping to suck a sensitive spot by my ear while I silently cursed wearing a halter dress.

"If we were alone, I'd rip that damned dress off you," he said huskily with a devilish grin.

"I might hold you to that, you know."

He laughed and took my hand and led me back to our table where the final golden glow of the sun slowly sank into the ocean. Votive candles centered on every table cast a romantic glow throughout the room.

The first course was already laid out on our table, but I couldn't focus on it. The entire meal was a blur as we picked at our food while getting to know each other better. It didn't help that my mind couldn't forget the feel of his lips on my neck and imagined what they would feel like elsewhere.

At the end of the night, Will wrapped his arm around me as we walked out into the cool salty sea air and got back into the limo. The divider was down and once the door was closed, Stewart looked at Will through the rear view mirror.

"Home, sir?"

Will looked at me and raised his eyebrows as if to silently ask me the same question. As much as I wanted to say yes, I couldn't.

"I really should be getting home. I have to be at work early, and I need to start working on my samples," I said. "They need to be perfect."

He smiled and nodded before reaching out for my hand and engulfing it in his.

"To Hargrove's, Stewart. Miss Hansen has to work in the morning."

"Yes sir," Stewart replied before sliding up the divider and steering the car into traffic.

"Thank you so much for such an amazing night. Everything was just perfect," I said, then summoned up my courage. "Will I see you again?"

"Yes. Before you know it," he said, smiling before kissing my forehead.

Chapter Nine
Deborah

Between being so busy with work and the pieces I needed to create for the final leg of the competition, the week after my dream date with Mr. Sexy flew by. It passed by so quickly that I barely noticed that Will never showed up at the store. I was so engrossed in everything that I didn't even care that he disappeared. I also took up lying to myself as a new hobby to support the old sarcastic one.

Still, not a day went by that I didn't think about my Mr. Sexy. I also spent that time kicking myself for not only forgetting to ask for his number, but for forgetting to give him mine. Unless he showed up at the store, I had no way of seeing him.

But then it happened. After that first week, I saw him more often. I never knew when he was coming in and sometimes it was only for a few minutes, but even those short visits became the highlight of my day. He always said he was just stopping by to say hi and that until I finished my samples, he would wait by the sidelines.

I couldn't believe how lucky I was. Not that I wanted him waiting, but knowing he was motivated me even more. No longer was I just creating the samples for the contest and myself. I had someone who was interested in what I was doing and supported me.

With every piece I made, I wondered what he would think of it. *Would he like it? Would he think I was sexy in it?* I went out of my way to make sure the samples were perfect and there wasn't a wrong or missed stitch anywhere, not only because I wanted to do my best for the contest, but because I wanted them to be flawless when I showed them to Will.

But why didn't he call? He found out my name somehow, surely if he wanted my number he would've gotten that, too. I was greedy and wanted more than just the work visits, but every time he showed up, I'd forget to slip him my number anyway.

While I drove myself crazy with questions, I focused on my creations. Not only did they keep me going, but I knew Will would show up eventually. I just never knew when.

Between working on my collection and waiting for Will, the month flew by and the day of my sample viewing arrived. I considered asking a friend to model my showstopper, the ocean and Tim Ross inspired chiffon gown, but at the last minute I changed my mind.

None of the other designers were using models, and I wanted to be sure that if I won, it would be on a level playing field. I didn't want anything I could point to for winning other than the strength of my collection.

Wearing the mid-calf circle skirt I created out of the silk-wool fabric with watercolor-style purple flowers on it, a purple silk camisole to match the flowers in the skirt, and a black shrug, I rode the elevator up to the corporate level once again, this time with my small rack of clothes.

I took a couple of deep breaths and waved my moist palms in the air as if that would take care of them. With my nerves on full speed, I was grateful for the slow elevator and glad I wore the cami to keep me cool.

Whenever I felt anxious, I tended to sweat. Someone once told me women don't sweat, as if by hearing that I would just magically stop. She said women glisten and glow. That certainly wasn't me. If women didn't sweat, then I was something other than a woman.

The last thing I needed was to sweat grossly during my presentation. I was confident my line would be the fashion forward yet wearable collection they were looking for, but my nerves always got the best of me.

As the doors opened, I pushed the rolling rack down the hall to Kylie's desk. She smiled widely when she saw me, like we were old friends.

"I've been looking forward to seeing your collection," she said. "Oooh, that's an amazing skirt! Did you make that, too?"

"Yes, thank you. I made everything I'm wearing. I try to only wear what I've designed."

I tried to peek at the list of candidates on her desk, but it was useless. While Kylie obviously liked gossiping, she also knew when it benefitted her to keep something secret.

"Are you trying to look?" she asked, grinning.

"Yes, I'm sorry, I was curious how many other designers made it this far."

"I'm sorry," she said as she wiggled four fingers in the air. "I really can't say."

I mouthed 'thank you' to her and looked over my designs one last time as Kylie disappeared into the conference room then popped her head out and waved me in.

Pushing the wheeled rack into the conference room, I suddenly felt calm. The samples were some of the best work I ever did, not only design-wise but craftsmanship, too. Everything I had worked for led to this moment, and I silently wished my grandma was still around to share it with me.

Amanda, Tim, and Claudine sat in the same seats as last time with notepads in front of each of them. They smiled at me warmly as I centered the rack, ready for any questions they might have.

"Good day, Miss Hansen," Tim said. "I have to say I've been looking forward to seeing your work all month."

"Thank you, I'm excited to share it with you. I've dreamt about having my own fashion line since

I was little. You'll notice elements from vintage styles, which I absolutely love, mixed with modern. All of my designs are made for real women like myself, but can be designed for a smaller girl and still be flattering."

As I spoke, I pointed to the different design elements I mentioned within each garment. They continued to smile and nod occasionally. None of them took many notes, but I did see Tim do a quick sketch of a dress with a similar style to one of my garments, which thrilled me. I couldn't believe something I created might have inspired him.

"How complete are these samples?" Amanda asked. "Your skill level seems very high. Can I get a closer look at that ruching?"

"All the samples are ready for fittings," I said as I laid the ocean blue gown on the table in front of them. "I did all the hand-ruching myself."

"Impressive," said Tim as the others nodded.

"So you'd be able to pack your samples and take them to...let's say hypothetically...Paris next week and then fit them on models?" Amanda asked.

"Hypothetically? Yes," I said.

"And in reality?"

"Unfortunately no. In reality, I need to work."

"And what if this was your work?"

"Please don't tease me."

Amanda leaned towards Tim as the three of them whispered. Confused, I tried to look busy rearranging the hangers while I waited to find out what was going on. They pointed at several items in my collection and then Amanda sat back.

"Paris Fashion Week is six days away and I planned for Hargrove's to show a collection, but there was a miscommunication and I have nothing but a reservation. Would you be able to leave in three days for Paris? You'll be gone for two weeks, and of course we'll cover all your expenses."

"Are you kidding me? Of course! I can leave now if you want."

She laughed then continued. "Congratulations, Deborah! I'm really looking forward to working with you on your next collection. Kylie will make all the arrangements for you and your assistant."

"Oh wow! Thank you! Thank you so much!" I said.

I ran up and hugged each of them again before quickly wheeling my rack of clothes out of the room before they realized what they did and changed their minds. My mind raced as I passed Kylie's desk, stopping to hug her too before I scrambled onto the elevator.

I had to tell someone! I hit the button for my floor, planning to go to the Men's department and find Dianna. I could burst, I was that excited!

I had so much to do. My mind raced as I wondered who could watch Trap for me and how I was going to afford the trip even though Hargrove's was paying for the big stuff. The elevator dinged as the doors opened. I stepped out, but one of the rack wheels got caught in the space between the floor and the elevator. I yanked the rack free and collided into someone.

"Shit! I'm so--" I began, then stopped as I realized it was Dianna. "I was just going to see you! I won! I won the contest!"

"I knew you'd win! Congratulations! I'm so happy for you."

"It was amazing! It all happened so fast. They loved everything and then asked me if I could get my samples model-ready for next week."

"Next week?"

"I'm going to Paris!"

"Bitch! I hate you," she joked. "Don't you get to bring an assistant? I know my way around a sewing machine, you know."

"I know you're joking, but if you're serious about knowing how to sew, I really will need help out there. I only have a few days once I get there to do fittings and all the alterations."

"Really? I am so there! I just need to clear it with the higher ups and make sure they have someone to cover for me. When do we leave?"

"In three days."

"I'm going to run up now to get everything squared away. Call me later when you find out all the details. Sure you won't change your mind? Maybe you'd like to bring someone else?"

"Someone else? No. I need help and we get along great. Who else would I bring?"

"Well, it is the city of love...maybe Mr. Sexy?"

"I don't have any way of getting in touch with him. Besides, I really need help out there. Plus I probably won't even see him before I go."

"If you say so. He's heading this way though," she said before jumping into the elevator and hitting the button repeatedly for the door to close.

As I turned towards the direction Dianna's eyes were focused on, Will appeared. With him dressed in a dark blue suit complemented by a sky blue button shirt, with the first couple of buttons undone and no tie, I couldn't take my eyes off him as he cut through a couple of departments on his way to me.

"You are hard to find," he said.

"Helps if I know when I'm being looked for."

"I'll pick you up at five tonight at your apartment. Bring a change of clothes, you'll be staying the night," he said then walked away.

I stood there with my jaw on the floor in shock, unable to speak. I wanted to say no and challenge him, but I couldn't. My mouth wouldn't even work to ask how he knew where I lived. The more forceful and demanding he became, the more I needed to have him and the more my body reacted to his gruff voice.

As I stepped outside, I looked around for him but he was gone. I looked for his long black stretch limo but found nothing. Carefully folding my collection and slipping the pieces into my old hard-sided suitcase, I left them in the car and headed back into the store.

Riding the escalator to the second level, I spotted exactly what I was looking for--lingerie. It was time to use my employee discount and credit card. Normally I slept in an oversized t-shirt, but if I was spending the night at Mr. Sexy's, I was hoping to do anything but sleep.

The lingerie department ran along the back wall of the second floor behind a white arch. One side had the basics--bras, panties, and slips in basic cotton, satin, and lace. I went to the other side, where several displays showed off their sexier items.

After deciding I wanted a babydoll, I looked through a few but couldn't find any in a large enough size.

"Can I help you with anything?" asked the saleswoman.

Her name tag said 'Natalie'. She had black and silver hair done in a bulletproof hairstyle she probably paid to get washed once a week. She had small wire-rim glasses perched at the end of her long thin nose, and she sucked in her cheeks as she waited for an answer.

"I'm looking for a babydoll in size 18 or 20."

She clucked and sighed as she quickly scanned the department. "Unfortunately dear, we don't stock much for big girls like you. I think there are a few things in clearance though. If you find anything in there, you're a lucky girl. I just added a few more items and there are some tremendous discounts."

"Thanks, I'll take a look," I said, feeling defeated.

I didn't expect to find anything pretty or sexy unless it was in a size that would fit my pinky, but I had to give it a shot. I didn't have enough time to go shopping if Will planned to pick me up at five. It had been a long time since I got myself lingerie ready for a man.

Looking through the racks of tightly packed undergarments, I became exceedingly disappointed until I saw a small tag with a 20 sticking up with several bright red lines going through the $400 price tag.

I followed the plastic tag down to the hanger and gently pulled out the cutest black babydoll set I had ever seen. Made with silk chiffon with chiffon pleats at the trim, the bra panel had a sheer geometric pattern with vintage floral motifs embroidered onto sheer tulle. To top it off, it came with a simple pair of black panties with ties at the hips. No wonder it cost so much!

Not wanting to try it on in the dressing room, I held it up against me. I thought it would fit, but what about the price? The lowest handwritten price on the tag was still $75. More than I could really afford to pay. Looking around the department, I spotted Natalie by the cash register and brought the babydoll over to her.

"Is the lowest price on here what it costs?" I asked.

She looked up at me and then down at the babydoll in my hands. "Oh goodness, I remember when this first came in. It's absolutely stunning," she said as she took it from me. Scanning the tag, the register beeped then flashed the price. "The clearance sale is 50% off the lowest price, then we also have an extra 20% off."

"Plus I'm an employee."

"Excellent! So another 10% off, that brings it to $27. That's a steal, dear. And trust me, I'm sure your boyfriend will find you good enough to eat in this!" she said with a smile.

"I sure hope so!" I said as I handed her my credit card and waited the longest couple of seconds of my life for the card to get approved.

***

Once I got home, I quickly tried the babydoll on. It fit perfectly. I put the receipt on top of my stack of bills and began calculating all my expenses for the month. Even with Will buying the fabric, I still had to spend some money on creating the samples. It was all money I needed to pay my rent.

The way I figured it, if I didn't have to pay rent while I was gone, I might actually have a little spending money in Paris. My landlord was always telling me how he was able to get higher rent for the apartments now that the neighborhood was turning around. Maybe he'd let me out of my lease.

I never liked the apartment anyway, it was the only thing I could afford though. Now, with winning the Hargrove's Designer Challenge, I'd be able to find a nicer apartment. Maybe one that didn't smell like the hot dog stand down the street.

It couldn't hurt to ask. And Mr. Annetti seemed more interested in how much he could make than keeping his tenants happy anyway. I had to call him.

"Hello?" Mr. Annetti's familiar gruff voice answered on the first ring.

"Hi, Mr. Annetti. It's Deborah Hansen in 4B."

"Is it the disposal again?"

"No, I wanted to talk about the lease."

"You want to flaunt that you're my last rent-control tenant?"

"I know how much that bothers you, so I'm willing to make you a deal."

"I'm listening."

"Let me out of my lease now, with my security deposit in full, and you can have my apartment."

"Hmm...I did just have someone call earlier looking for a rental in the new price range. How soon can you be out?"

"You can have it back this weekend," I said.

"It's a deal. I'll even hand you your security check when I get your keys."

"Great! It's a deal then. Thanks, Mr Annetti!"

Hanging up, I felt better even though it meant I'd be homeless when I got back from Paris. I'd figure something out. My phone beeped with a voicemail message from Hargrove's.

"Please don't say they changed their minds," I said as I waited for the message to begin.

"Hey Deborah, Kylie from Hargrove's. You'll never believe this, but you'll be traveling on the owner's jet." Her voice lowered before she continued. "Ends up he's got a speaking engagement or something out there. I'm jealous! Anyway, you leave Saturday. Make sure you get me your assistant's name so he knows to expect her, too. Talk soon!"

A private jet? I immediately called Dianna, unable to believe my luck. I didn't even wait for her to say hello. I just started talking as soon as I heard her answer.

"Oh my God oh my God, Dianna! We're going on the owner's jet!"

"Ooh, swanky! But I can't go! Such a shame I'll miss that. I'm going to have to take a flight the next day. I couldn't get anyone to cover for me until the next shift."

"Oh no! So I'll be traveling alone with him? I just hope he's not too much of an old fart. If I have to share a plane with him for all those hours, he better be up for talking. I know I'll be too excited to sleep."

"I hear some of those jets have TV and everything. You won't have to talk to him. He might not even sit with you. It's an entire jet, you know."

"Oh right, duh. What was I thinking?" I said, laughing. "I'm just not really here. Mr. Sexy is picking me up soon. He told me I'll be staying the night so my head is...well, you know."

"Oooh, I love a man who knows what he wants. You realize I'm going to need lots of details. And as you tell me, I'll be pretending it's happening to me. Have fun!"

"Will do!" I said. "I'll call Kylie tomorrow and tell her you're my assistant. I'm sure she'll be able to arrange for a flight for you."

"She'd better! I can't wait!"

Laughing, I got her off the phone and pushed all the things I needed to do to get ready for my trip to the back of my mind. Right now, I had to focus on looking good for Will and nothing else.

Chapter Ten

Deborah

I packed a small overnight bag with the babydoll, a change of clothes, and some necessities, but I kept thinking about how surreal it was that I was going to spend the night like this. What happened to romance? Maybe I was over-thinking things. It wouldn't be the first time.

Scratching Trap on the top of his head, I remembered I needed someone to watch him while I was away. Between work and school, I never made that many friends. I never had time to socialize. Ashley Boone was the only person I knew who might take Trap in.

Checking the clock, I figured I could manage a quick call before Will showed up. I dialed her number while crossing my fingers for luck.

"Hey Ashley, it's Deborah."

"Oh hi! How are you doing? I was just thinking about you the other day. Joshua told me how well things were going with you at Hargrove's."

"Well, they just got even better. I won their Annual Designer Challenge, and they want me to show my collection at Fashion Week in Paris."

"That's incredible! Congratulations! I knew you'd win! There's no way that store has anyone else as talented as you."

"You're sweet, thank you," I said. "I really hate to do this, but I was wondering if I could ask you a favor?"

"Of course, whatever you want."

"I don't know if you remember, but I have a cat named Trap. I'm leaving for Paris in a few days for two weeks and have no one else to take care of him. Would you mind if I brought him over? I know it's a long time and you're busy so if it's too much please, just say no and I'll understand."

"It's no bother at all. Of course I'll take care of him while you're gone. Don't worry about him."

"Thank you so much, Ash! I really do owe you."

"Then make me something!" she said and laughed.

"Okay, okay! I promise, after I get back," I said as I peeked out the window and saw a long black limousine pull up in front of the apartment building. "I'm sorry to cut this short, but I gotta go. My date is here."

"Ooh, date? I want to hear all about him when you drop off Trap."

"Yes ma'am! Thanks again, Ashley. You're a lifesaver."

Hanging up, I quickly ran to give myself a quick once over in the bathroom mirror. I decided to go casual and wear jeans with a low cut dark orange v-neck tunic with my favorite pair of strappy brown sandals.

The buzzer rang and without waiting for him to say anything, I grabbed my things and hit the intercom. "I'm coming down now," I said, suddenly self-conscious of where I lived and not wanting him to see the tiny studio apartment I called home.

Making sure that Trap had enough food and water, I left a nightlight on for him then stepped out into the hall and right into Will.

"Shit, sorry! This isn't the first time I've done this. I'm a bit of a pro collider," I said as I tried to quickly pull the door closed behind me.

Without a word, Will pushed the door open and stepped inside. His long stride made easy work of my apartment. I followed him, dropping my things on the floor by the entrance.

"What are you doing?" I asked.

"Looking around."

"I can see that. The thing is I didn't invite you in. Can we just go?"

"Why don't you want me to see where you live? I'm taking you to see my home."

I didn't answer. He was baiting me, and I wasn't in the mood. Instead, I picked up my things and walked out. I couldn't take him looking around and seeing how poor I was.

"Lock the door when you're done and don't let the cat out," I said as I began wondering what his problem was.

Did he really need to control everything so much that he couldn't just accept not knowing one small thing like where I lived? It slowly dawned on me that I hardly knew anything about him. For all I knew, he could be a designer, too. Or maybe a crazed serial killer who murdered unsuspecting tailors.

"This is ridiculous!" I said aloud as I entered my apartment again. "Will?" I called out. "Will?"

Trap meowed as he jumped off the couch. Will had taken his blue suit jacket off and folded it over the arm of the couch. He sat beside it, his long legs stretched out in front of him.

"You found me," he said, grinning.

"Not a big place. Can we go now?"

"Why? This is a great little place."

"You've got to be kidding me. It's a shit hole," I said as I looked around, noticing the cracks on the wall and the peeling paint by the window.

"It's your own place though. I've lived in the same house most of my life."

"If you don't like where you live, then move."

"No, I have to stay," he said as his face grew hard. "Let's go."

He got up and walked past me and out the door without a word. I grabbed my bags again and locked the door as I rushed to catch up with him in the elevator. I hit the stop button.

"What is your problem?" I demanded. "I don't even know why I followed you. I should just let you leave, I don't need this."

"Then go."

He looked straight ahead, his expression empty of any feeling. Somehow I felt bad for him.

He was taking me to his home. I knew he was very private, and something about his home seemed to hurt him. He didn't act like it, but I couldn't help but think he needed me.

"You can really be an asshole sometimes, you know," I said as I hit the down button and let the elevator doors close. I thought I saw him smile, but it was so brief I might have imagined it.

Stewart stood beside the limo and opened the door for us as we left my apartment building. He took my bags and placed them in the trunk while we got into the car.

"I'm sorry," Will said quietly. "I'm glad you're coming. I don't get many guests."

Somehow I knew that was an understatement. I looked out the window as we drove, watching as we left the city.

"I hate to admit this to you," I said as I watched the passing scenery, "but every day I hope you'll show up at the store again. I hate that I don't have a way to reach you."

"Sorry, I should have left you my number. I would have been there more often, but I had a lot of business to wrap up," he said then looked out the window. "This is it."

I leaned over to look out his window and saw nothing but trees behind a tall stone fence. The car slowed and I saw we had stopped in front of an old wrought iron gate, which slowly opened.

"This is where you live?" I asked, stunned.

He nodded. "My mother found that gate on a trip to France. There are things like that all over the property. She had a great eye and saw beauty everywhere." He looked down, visibly upset, before his face turned to stone again.

We were quiet during the short drive to his mansion. It looked like something out of a movie with its gothic design and enormity. I thought places like this didn't really exist, at least not as people's homes.

Once we were inside, I couldn't stop looking around. There were oil paintings and sculptures everywhere. Even a suit of shining armor. I felt like I had walked into a museum.

"I can't believe this is your home."

He shrugged and picked up my bags, which Stewart had placed on the floor. "I'll show you to your room," he said.

"My room? But I thought..."

Laughing, he shook his head. "Maybe I'm a little old fashioned. It's not that I don't want to, of course, but I know I can be a little demanding. This way, if you think I'm being an asshole again, you have space to yourself."

I burst out laughing as I followed him up a large curved marble staircase. Upstairs was more homey. At the top of the stairs was a loft area with a balcony that overlooked the expansive living space below. A honey-colored berber carpet covered the floor along the hall, and the only hint of the gothic styling of the rest of the mansion were the oversized double doors we passed.

Towards the end of one of the long halls, Will dramatically opened both doors of one of the rooms, then stepped aside as he put down my bags.

"Are you going to enter?" he asked, noticing my frozen state.

"I...I..." I tried to speak, but words wouldn't come out. Just the little glimpse of what I saw was too much.

Taking one of my hands in his, with his other hand on the small of my back, he led me into the room. His wood-spice scent mixed with the smell of new furniture and fresh paint, and I had to stop again when my legs felt weak.

The room was easily twice the size of my entire apartment. At the center of the room was a king-sized bed with a plum upholstered headboard. The bedding was reminiscent of the fabric I made the skirt out of with watercolor purple flowers. Next to me was a small sitting area with several plush almond-colored chairs with plum throw pillows. Light poured into the sitting area from French doors that opened to a small balcony overlooking a flower garden and a view of the valley.

"What is all this? I mean it's beautiful. It's the bedroom of my dreams and even in my favorite color, but...I just don't understand," I said as I tore my eyes away from the room to look up into his smiling face.

"I knew you'd like it. I know we're both busy and I don't get to see you nearly as much as I would like, so I wanted to give you a room here. I want you to move in, but it's up to you. You can stay here whenever you like."

Speechless, I hugged him tight and felt his strong body slowly relax as he stroked my hair and held me close.

"Sir, dinner is ready," Stewart said from the hall.

"Seems like we're always getting interrupted," Will said as he let me go and we followed Stewart back downstairs and into the formal dining room.

The focal point of the dining room was a long walnut table that could easily seat twenty people. Noticing two settings at either ends of the table, I started to laugh.

"Okay, now you've got to be kidding me," I said.

Will looked at me for a second before laughing, too. "I thought you'd like this. Find it all impressive and formal. Don't women like that? It's worked before." He grinned slyly.

I rolled my eyes at him. "I don't know, maybe some do, but I think this is ridiculous," I said, trying to stop laughing as I imagined us trying to have a conversation from across the length of the table. "Do you normally eat here?"

"Of course, all the time." He was serious for a moment and then laughed. "I've actually only been in this room a handful of times. Stewart and I usually eat together in the kitchen."

"Then let's eat in there. I mean, you saw my apartment, I really don't need all this. And I hope Stewart will be joining us. If you normally eat with him and I'm going to be here more often, then I should get to know him better."

The kitchen looked like it was suited more for a restaurant than a house. With a walk-in pantry the size of my apartment and a walk-in refrigerator and freezer, I was surprised to find them mostly empty.

I set a small chef block style table as Stewart served and Will opened a bottle of wine. Unable to keep my curiosity at bay any longer, I started asking questions.

"Will, you said you've lived here all of your life. Is it just the two of you here?"

"We had a smaller home before, but I was little so I don't remember it. My father made some wise business decisions and that cemented our wealth. This property was a gift to my mother, who always loved it. Stewart and I are the only people who live here. There are some housekeepers and gardeners, but they come and go."

"And how long have you known Stewart?"

"Almost my whole life. After my parents passed, it was Stewart who raised me. He used to drive for my father."

"Oh? I had no idea."

"Yes, that's true," Stewart said. "Will's parents didn't have any family. Luckily I had been named guardian or Will would have become a ward of the state."

"So you're like a father to him," I said.

"No, not really. I was young myself when it happened, only in my twenties. Will was eight at the time so if anything, I was more of an older brother. I knew nothing about raising a child, but I swore to protect him."

"I'm sure that was hard on both of you," I said as I looked over at Will, who set glasses of white wine on the table.

"It was," he said coldly. "Now I think we should move on."

Stewart shot Will a mean look, but nothing else was said. We sat quietly, eating roasted chicken and potato gratin with a rich cheddar cheese and jalapeño sauce that was delicious. I wanted to ask if Stewart cooked since I didn't see anyone else in the giant mansion, but I didn't want to upset Will any further with my questions.

The silence lasted the rest of the meal. I couldn't take it anymore, so once I was done eating, I got up to excuse myself.

"I think I'll head up to bed," I said. "I need to get up early to pack my apartment for storage and get ready for Paris."

"Paris?" Stewart asked.

"Oh yes. I won the design competition at Hargrove's. Not only that, but I'm showing my collection at Fashion Week in Paris!"

"Congratulations! I'm surprised Will didn't tell me."

"That's my fault, with everything going on, I completely forgot to tell him. And Will, I would've never been able to win without you helping me with the fabrics."

"You did it all on your own, Deborah," Will said. "It was your designs and skill that won, I did nothing."

"I couldn't have created my samples without you. You have no idea how broke I am right now." I felt embarrassed admitting it, no matter how true it was. "Anyway, I have a lot to do in the next couple of days. Thank you for everything. Good night!"

I left them and tried to figure out my way back upstairs to my bedroom, but I got lost. Turning back, I entered what I thought was the dining room so I could retrace my steps but entered a library instead.

The room was dark with mahogany floor-to-ceiling built in bookcases and a desk the size of my car at the end of the room. On the desk was an old push button telephone and a calendar from twenty-five years ago. The desk hadn't been used in all that time.

Above the desk was a large oil portrait of a small family--father, mother, and son--all with dark brown hair and impeccably dressed standing in front of a Christmas tree with piles of gifts all around.

They were an attractive family and I knew they had to be related to Will somehow, so I got closer to the painting. With genuine looking smiles on their faces, it was obvious this was a happy family. And the boy, with his hazel eyes with green flecks, was undeniably Will.

"I knew you'd get lost," Will said, startling me.

"I should've asked for directions, but honestly they probably wouldn't have helped," I said, laughing. "Are these your parents?"

He nodded. "Yes, that was taken shortly before..." his voice trailed off.

I wanted to ask him how it happened, but by the quick flash of green in his eyes and how his face suddenly hardened, I knew I wouldn't get an answer. Instead, I wrapped my arms around him.

He held me tight, as if everything depended on that hug, and then kissed the top of my head as he exhaled.

"Come, I'll take you to your room. I want to talk to you privately anyway," he said.

"What is it?" I asked once we entered my room.

Will walked over to one of the chairs and patted the top of it. "Please, sit," he said, then he opened the French doors, letting in a warm breeze and the sweet scent of roses and honeysuckle.

"Did I do something? Is something wrong?"

"No. It's just...you said you were going to put your things into storage. I'd really like you to consider keeping them here. Even if after you return from Paris and you decide to get another apartment, I'll feel better knowing your things are here. Where it's safe."

"What is it with all this safety? Is someone after you?"

"I don't know. It's been like this most of my life. There have been threats, incidents. It's why I've always closed myself off from everyone. Until now." He walked back over to me and sat on the edge of the seat in front of me and took my hands.

"The world is a bad place, Deborah. But you can always be safe here."

I wanted to say I didn't understand. I needed to know why between him and Stewart, they always seemed to be concerned about safety. But I could see in his eyes that he was telling me the truth and trusted me. Learning to trust someone was hard for me too, and here Will was, letting me into his life in a way he never had with anyone else. I was in no place to question him.

"I know I'm safe with you, Will. I wouldn't be here otherwise."

Leaning forward, he kissed my lips, and any reservations I had slipped away. I wrapped my arms around his shoulders and he picked me up and carried me to the bed.

While I hadn't been with a man in a long time, I never forgot that feeling of nervousness. Worrying if my body looked okay, or if he would think what I covered up with clothes was too big for him undressed. It didn't matter what size I was, I was always insecure about myself naked.

As he sat me down on the bed, my heart fluttered in anticipation. His fingers slid into my hair as he kissed me again, this time lingering before dipping his tongue into my mouth. The warmth of his mouth on mine spread through my body. When his lips left mine, I couldn't wait to find out where they'd go next.

"Sleep well, Deborah," he said before kissing my forehead.

I closed my eyes, expecting his lips to move further down, but heard the sound of his footsteps leaving my room instead. Sitting up, I stared at his back as he left my room.

"You've got to be kidding me," I said. "This has to be a joke."

It wasn't. I must have sat there for fifteen minutes waiting for him to come back. At first I tried a sexy pose for him to find me in, but I felt ridiculous. Then I thought I'd try the Sleeping Beauty approach. I laid down with my eyes closed pretending to be asleep for when he returned. He never did. And I think I really did fall asleep for a few minutes.

Sitting up in the bed, I couldn't believe my luck. I knew he was just being a gentleman, but couldn't he do that tomorrow? As I got out of bed, I figured maybe it was for the best. I did have to get up early and I had a lot to do.

Fuck that! This was Mr. Sexy we're talking about. The man who almost whipped it out in the middle of a department store. I didn't know when I'd get to see him again. And I wanted him. Now. I didn't go through the trouble of buying lingerie and shaving for nothing.

Opening my bag, I dumped everything onto the bed, figuring that was the quickest way to find the babydoll I bought. I quickly undressed, slipped it on, tied the bows of the panties at my hips, then looked at myself in the mirror. *Hmm, not bad.* The sheer panel on the top made it look like my breasts were exposed except for the well-placed embroidery over my nipples. It was a nice touch. Plus, with my habit of showing off the girls, it seemed fitting.

Now to get my man. Opening the door to my bedroom, I peeked down the hall and realized I had no idea where Will could be. Roaming the mansion half naked wasn't high on my list, especially after getting lost once already. I needed to think.

As I leaned against the door, my eyes were drawn to the balcony. Could I be that lucky? I stepped out onto the balcony and looked at the surrounding balconies. Nothing. Just then, I heard the click of a glass onto a table. Underneath me was a flagstone patio. Stretching over the balcony enough, I was able to see Will's legs crossed with an ankle on his knee.

Running my fingers through my hair one last time, I entered the hall and padded barefoot back along the carpeted hallway to the staircase. Crossing my arms over my chest in case I ran into Stewart, I went down to the first level and found a similar hall to the one with the bedrooms, only with marble flooring instead of carpeting. Guessing which of the doors to open based on where my bedroom was, I stepped inside a room.

The room was a total man cave. All the furniture was dark and large but didn't close off the room completely since the back wall was made entirely of glass. Will sat on a wide upholstered outdoor chair, his back towards me. A small table was beside him with the empty glass I heard before. Summoning all of my courage, I leaned against the doorway with my best come hither look.

"You know, you never let me finish measuring your inseam. I was just about to demonstrate that special technique."

He turned around with a confused expression that quickly disappeared. Slowly his eyes traveled down my body, then back up again.

"Now it's my turn to be surprised," he said. "And what a nice surprise it is."

"You left me hanging."

"I was being a gentleman. It's bad enough I told you you were spending the night. I didn't want you feel like--"

"Like I might get lucky?"

He laughed, and I carefully walked on the flagstone over to him. The sun had almost completed its descent into the valley, casting the last of its orange glow against the glass wall of the house. Seeing my reflection in the glass, I thought of our date at The Breezes.

"I've been doing a lot of thinking," I said as I stood in front of him. "And I've realized you're just a tease. There's that time at the store, then at the restaurant you threatened to rip my dress off but didn't, and now tonight."

"I know you're teasing, but you have no idea how many times I've thought about how sexy you'd look naked," he said, his voice husky as he moved to the edge of his seat. "I can see I was right."

He pulled me towards him, his hands hot through the thin fabric of my lingerie. After kissing my chin softly, his lips moved to my neck where he sucked and kissed as my core throbbed.

Standing to the side of his long outstretched legs, I couldn't help but think about how badly I wanted to see what was hidden in his pants. I reached for the front of his pants, my fingers sliding over the material, feeling his hardened member underneath.

I made quick work opening his pants, exposing his blue striped boxers. Feeling like a kid at Christmas, I bit my lip as I unwrapped his large member. Will's fingers wrapped around the black straps of my babydoll.

"No, not yet," I said as my fingers moved over his stiff manhood.

Will leaned back into the chair as I wrapped my hand around him and slowly stroked up and over his meaty head, a little wet with pre-cum. Needing to taste him, I lowered my mouth and ran my tongue along his shaft, repeating the journey my hand had been on.

As I reached his head, I flicked my tongue over the opening, tasting a salty sweet drop before sliding him into my mouth. Will groaned and dug his fingers into my fleshy hips. Finding the bows that tied my panties on, he pulled at them both and let my panties drop to the ground.

Bent over, with my legs spread and no panties on, I felt naked but in control. I slowly lowered my mouth further down him, his cock filling my mouth as I felt his hand follow the curve of my ass as his thick fingers neared my slick folds.

I slid him out of my mouth again and looked up at Will as I teased his head with my tongue. His fingertips slid over my wetness then between my lower lips. I had a hard time focusing on what I was doing when two of his fingers grazed my clit, causing me to jump slightly.

I couldn't help it. Between how long it had been for me and being there with my Mr. Sexy, my body tingled and throbbed with heightened sensitivity. Unable to hold myself back any longer, I straddled him, placing my knees on either side of his hips.

Giving me his crooked, mischievous smile, he slipped his hands under the babydoll and caressed my hips as I positioned myself over his rod. As I pressed his tip to my entrance, I had to control myself. I wanted to feel him inside me so badly.

Gasping as I slowly lowered myself onto his thick cock, my core began throbbing intensely, pulsing up my spine. Will wrapped his hands around my hips.

We moved slowly at first, enjoying the first taste of each other's bodies. I leaned down to kiss him, and our tongues hungrily explored each other's mouths as his hands took over the pace of my hips.

Thrusting faster, his fingers digging pleasurably into my skin, I ripped open his shirt. As I pushed it down past his strong shoulders, I kissed the muscle that flexed as his hands pulled my body onto him.

Shifting my body a little, his member began stroking my g-spot, sending shivers up my spine. As I let out a soft moan, Will slowed down, letting the throbbing sensation in my core build.

He kissed along my shoulders then used his teeth to pull down the delicate straps of my babydoll, revealing my breasts. His warm tongue passed over my nipples, drawing circles, before he blew cold air onto them. The combination of him and the cooling night air made them even harder. I sighed with pleasure as he relieved them by sucking slowly.

My body trembled as the pressure in me reached its climax. Gasping for breath, I clutched tightly onto Will as my hips thrust onto him a couple more times before I let go and felt goose bumps run up my back and into my hair.

Feeling my body tremble and tighten around him, Will let out a growl before erupting inside me. With my body spent, he slid my hips back and forth as he came. I felt so sensitive there, but it felt so good I didn't want him to stop. Biting his shoulder, I waited for the tingling sensation to slow before I collapsed against him, both of us out of breath.

Will stroked my back softly as I laid on top of him in the moonlight. Glad Will didn't have any neighbors, I pulled up the straps of my babydoll.

"You're a gorgeous woman, Deborah. I know you think of yourself as a big girl, but you know what? That just means there's more of you to kiss, more of you to touch and feel under my hands and mouth."

Blood rushed to my cheeks, making them burn as I imagined what he could do to me. Being with Will was different than any other man I had been with. He looked at me like I was a small bunny and he was a wolf. I wanted him to devour me. Will had the ability to make me feel so sexy, I thought I could do anything in the world.

As our lips met once again, Will stood up, holding onto me with my legs now wrapped around him. I felt his manhood underneath me begin to harden again, and I giggled like a school girl.

He carried me up to my bedroom and laid us both down on the bed. His lips moved to my neck and I shivered, waiting for where he would go next. I doubted I'd get much sleep that night, but I could care less. Mr. Sexy definitely lived up to his name.

***

I was alone when I woke as the sun came through the windows. As I rubbed my eyes, glad Will wouldn't see what I looked like first thing in the morning, I noticed a small purple plaid luggage set sitting in the middle of the room. *That wasn't there last night,* I thought. As I got closer to the set, I noticed a small piece of paper on top of the largest piece--a roller bag.

Deborah,

I'm sorry to leave you alone, but I had some last minute business to take care of. I hope you'll enjoy using these on your trip to Paris. I had them custom ordered after our first date. I knew you'd win.

I don't know when I'll be able to see you again in the next couple of days, but I will definitely see you before your flight.

I'll be thinking about you.
With Love,
Will

I couldn't stop smiling as I read the note. I loved that he had such faith in me that he ordered the set knowing I'd win. Just thinking about him again made my body tingle with excitement. *With Love.* I wondered what it meant, and if it meant anything, but I'd have to obsess about it another time. I had too much to do in the next two days before the trip to Paris Fashion Week.

Chapter Eleven

Deborah

After spending the night with Will, the next two days flew by. I dropped Trap off at Ashley and Xander's the day before and she texted me earlier that he was doing fine. Happy to hear he adjusted without having me around, I knew I'd be able to enjoy my two weeks away.

The only thing on my mind was my Mr. Sexy. I wished he could come with me to Paris. After all, it was the City of Love. I didn't even ask him to join me though. At least he said he'd see me before the flight.

That was a good and bad thing. Normally for a flight I'd just wear something really comfortable, especially with how long the flight to Paris was. But between meeting Mr. Hargrove and seeing Will, I needed to look good. I chose a dark red silk wraparound skirt with an embroidered vine that wrapped up one side and paired it with a black cami with lace accents. On top of that, I wore a short black jacket that I thought looked cute with the outfit.

Looking around my apartment, I thought about how much I'd miss the tiny dump. It was my first apartment on my own and I knew I'd always look back on it with a smile.

With everything packed in boxes, it looked even smaller. Stewart told me he'd arrange for all my things to be brought over to the mansion. Glad to not have to worry about that or pay for storage, I considered those to be the icing on the cake. *The cake being living with my very own Mr. Sexy!*

It was all very surreal to me how quickly things went from my graduating, to taking the job at Hargrove's and meeting Will, to winning the competition and now moving in with him. The reasonable part of me thought things were moving too fast and I was going to get hurt. The other part of me knew I'd regret not doing it.

I felt so comfortable with Will, I knew he was my forever. Just being with him, even when he shut down and wouldn't speak, I was more myself than I ever was with anyone else. Even though I hadn't said the words yet, I knew I wasn't falling in love with him, I had already fallen.

I read the note he left me one more time. I kept it folded in my pocket these past two days and must have read it hundreds of times by now. Obsessing over it like I was, I knew I was reading too much into it, but I couldn't help it. He signed it "with love".

Did he mean it? Was that his way of saying he loved me? Or did he always sign everything "with love"?

While I drove myself crazy with the questions, the honking of a car horn sounded from outside. Rushing to the window, I hoped to see Will there, even though I knew it was the cab ready to take me to the airport.

Where was he? He said he'd see me before my flight.

Patience wasn't one of my strong points. The cab blew its horn again, this time more insistently, proving I wasn't the only impatient person there at the moment.

Lifting the strap of the shoulder bag Will bought me onto my shoulder, I then grabbed the handle of the matching roller bag with the toiletries bag attached to it and pulled it towards the door. Lastly, I grabbed the wardrobe bag that had all my samples for the collection with extra fabrics in case

I needed them. Hargrove's said I could ship it, but there was no way I was letting all that hard work out of my sight.

Looking around the apartment one last time, my eyes got misty. *Come on, Deborah! No time to be emotional!* I silently said good-bye to the place before locking the door and beginning the first step of my new life.

***

Having been at the airport for two hours, I officially lost what was left of my patience. Will wasn't answering his phone or his texts. I was sure he regretted giving his number to the crazy woman he asked to move in.

"Where are you?" I asked the phone. "You said you'd be here."

Frustrated, I texted him again. *Where are you?* I stood at the gate looking at the Hargrove's large private jet. Noticing an attractive woman with brown hair pulled back in a ponytail wearing a red uniform the same color as the Hargrove's logo approaching me, I knew my time was up.

"Miss Hansen, you really should board now," the flight attendant said to me.

"Alright, alright," I said, looking at my cell phone and willing it to ring or beep or do anything to indicate a message from Will.

She grabbed the handle of the roller bag and I followed her through the doors and outside. As we walked on the tarmac to the plane, I kept looking around, hoping Will would magically appear. I hated leaving without saying good-bye.

Climbing the steps to board the plane, I had to hold onto my skirt as it blew around me. Once I got to the top of the steps, I turned and looked around one more time, silently praying for even a few moments with him. Nothing.

My heart ached. I wondered if he just wanted to sleep with me and that was it. Maybe it wasn't as good for him as it was for me. I really thought we had something though. *And what about "with love"?*

Sighing deeply, I entered the plane, and it immediately reminded me of Will's limousine, except this had caramel leather seats. It even had a row of seats connected together like a long couch.

As the flight attendant rolled my bag to the back, I saw Mr. Hargrove was already on board and probably pissed at having to wait for me. His back was towards me, but he immediately reminded me of Will. *That's it, I've lost it! Now I'm seeing things!*

He wore a navy suit that looked like the Tom Ford suit my Mr. Sexy tried on before I knew him as Will. He had his hands in his pants pockets in a way that showed he wore suits so often, he was comfortable in them. It wasn't something I noticed in a lot of men. Lastly, he had on a fedora that matched the suit perfectly. The hat was rakishly tilted a bit to one side as if it had a personality of its own.

I couldn't tear my eyes away. Standing in an aisle, I set my bag down and stared. Positive I was certifiably insane and going to spend my time in Paris seeing Will in every man wearing a suit, I texted him one last time. *I really hoped to see you before I left.*

Within seconds Mr. Hargrove pulled his cell phone out, and I dropped mine. *It couldn't be. He would've told me. He should have told me.*

"Will?" I choked out. He turned around, his lips in that crooked smile I suddenly wanted to hate. "Are you...?" I couldn't even say it. I didn't want to even think it.

He walked down the aisle and stood in front of me. As he gently touched my cheek, I felt all my anger slip away. *No! I should be angry!*

"Deborah Hansen," he said as he looked into my eyes and I tried very hard not to melt, "allow me to introduce myself. I am William Hargrove King, the Third."

"How could you do this to me?!" I pushed him away as another flight attendant closed the door.

"What are you talking about?" he asked.

"You lied to me! We've been dating for a month and you never thought to tell me? You knew all along that I was a contestant in the Hargrove's Designer Challenge, and you never once told me who you really were! I should've known I didn't win on my own. I only won so you could fuck me!"

"No! It's not like that at all. I'm not even involved in the contest. I'm only here because I wanted to get away with you."

"Don't talk to me! I have to get off this plane."

"I'm sorry, Miss," the flight attendant said. "We're cleared for take-off. You need to sit down and buckle up. Now!"

"How could you, Will? I can't show my collection now. I'm a fraud! I can't get off this plane and have everyone know I'm the owner's fucking girlfriend. Am I even that?"

"Calm down. You're making a bigger deal out of this than it needs to be," he said as he sat next to me.

"No! Go sit somewhere else. I don't even want to see you right now. You have no idea what you did! Everything I worked for, I thought I did all of this on my own, and it turns out all I did was flirt with the right guy. Please, just leave me alone."

He walked to the front of the plane and sat down without looking back at me. I knew I hurt him, but at that moment I didn't care. Anger fueled me. I didn't know what to do. I'd have to cancel the show and my dream of showing a collection at Fashion Week. All that hard work had been wasted. No one would ever take me seriously now.

Chapter Twelve

Will

Getting up, I walked towards the front of the plane and sat down, leaving Deborah hurt and seething with rage in her seat. This was why I didn't have relationships. They were too complicated. My one-night stands were much easier.

Thinking about the faceless women who had shared my bed, I felt a bit sad. Not that I regretted any of them, of course. I just didn't want Deborah to become one of them. She meant more to me than I cared to admit, and that worried me. I purposefully secluded myself not out of fear of danger but out of fear of loss.

Twenty-Five Years Ago

The Canyon Cove Christmas Extravaganza ended with heavy red velvet curtains closing at the foot of the stage. The annual show billed itself as "spectacular" and never disappointed. Ending the show was a nativity scene with live animals and the most brilliant star shining upon them that any eight-year-old had ever seen. Even me, and by then my parents had taken me into the city to see the show the past four years in a row.

"What did you think of the show, Will?" my dad asked as he did every year.

William Hargrove King, Jr., my father and namesake, wore a permanent smile. It wasn't fake, he was always happy and did what he could to make others around him happy, too. It was his idea to begin the annual trip into the city to see the Christmas Extravaganza, and he enjoyed it as much as I did.

"It was awesome, Dad! Even better than last year!" I replied.

"I'm glad you had fun," he said as he mussed my hair as the three of us walked up the aisle towards the lobby doors to the exit.

I walked between my parents, both of them holding my hands. We were dressed up like most of the other people who watched the show. Dad was handsome with his brown and silver hair combed back, dressed in a black pinstriped suit with a red tie. Mom turned heads in a simple dress the same shade of red as the tie, her dark hair pinned back over her ear with a small barrette she always wore to keep her wavy brown hair out of her eyes.

Even then, I felt comfortable wearing a suit. Dressed in a child's version of my father's suit, I looked like a miniature version of him. I wouldn't have had it any other way. I looked up to my father and wanted to be just like him.

As we bundled ourselves in our coats before stepping out into the cold, I looked at our reflection in the gold mirrored walls lining the entry. We were happy. We were a family. We were also the wealthiest people in town.

Exiting the warmth of the building, the cold air stung my lungs. Stewart, our driver, left the limo running at the curb and cut a path through the crowd for us. He was lanky in his navy driver's uniform and while I always thought he was old, I later learned what was old to a child differs greatly from reality.

Stewart's dark blond hair fell into his eyes before he pushed it back and under his driver's cap. Only in his late twenties, Stewart already lived many lives and had a history I would never fully know.

"Sir, I still think you need to hire security," he said to my father as he guided us through the thick throng of people waiting outside the theater. "A man in your position--"

"In my position?" my father asked.

"Yes, your wealth--"

"Wealth means nothing. I wasn't always rich. I grew up not far from here, as you know. Before Hargrove's became a household name, I knew what it was like to wonder where our next meal was coming from." He looked around at the crowd. "Why would anyone hurt me?"

Stewart sighed. "The economy does strange things to people. You know I trust no one. And you hired me for protection."

"For my wife and child, not myself. You know better than to bring this up in front of them," my father said through clenched teeth.

Silenced, Stewart opened the car door for us. Dad looked around at the crowd again, then to us, his small family.

"I want to show you something. I haven't mentioned this to you before because I didn't want you to worry, but I know this is the right decision for our company," my dad said as he looked into my mother's light blue eyes. "Let's go for a walk."

"But sir--"

"No. This is between my family and I. We're going alone. This is about the future. Like I said before, we're safe. This is my old hang out. Do not follow us. I expect the car to be right where it is now."

Stewart nodded and stepped out of the way, letting my dad lead us down the block.

"Where are we going, Bill?" My mother asked, her voice filled with worry. "It's late. Couldn't you show us another time? Maybe when it's not so dark?"

We were only a block away from the theater, but its bright lights didn't make it down the street that far. The moon was covered by thick clouds, and the only light came from the dim street lamps that graced the corners.

"I grew up not far from here," my father said. "Across the street was the ice cream shop I'd stop by after school."

While we walked, my father continued reminiscing. The street grew quieter as we passed less people, and suddenly it felt like we were alone in this old part of the big city. Surrounding us were old tenements, run down and uncared for. The buildings had a strange mixture of sadness and despair as they looked down upon us.

"The neighborhood changed after I left. These old buildings once had their own personalities, but after decades of neglect, they've begun to crumble."

"Dad, I'm cold. I want to go home," I whined.

"Soon. You need to see this. It's your future," he said before pointing up to the top of the building across the street where a large banner with 'Hargrove's Fine Department Store Coming Soon' emblazoned across it. "None of these buildings can be saved. They've been destroyed by time, but I wanted to give back to the community where I grew up."

I turned around, thinking I heard movement in the darkness, but I couldn't see anything. My mother was shivering and pulled me closer to tighten the wool scarf around my neck. Suddenly a deep, slurred voice came from within the shadow of a doorway.

"Pretty people like you shouldn't be here."

My mother pulled me closer to her. She still shivered, but I knew her chill had been replaced with fear.

"We were just leaving. Weren't we, Bill?" she said as she gently nudged my father while holding me as if I was attached.

Because my mother held me so close, I couldn't really see the man who stepped out of the shadows. I definitely could smell him though--a rank mixture of alcohol and sweat. Every time he spoke, my blood turned cold.

"N-n-now wait a minute here," he said, stumbling over his words. "I know you. Your face. I've seen you on TV. You're the reason me and hundreds of others were run outta here. You bought our homes so you could build a ridiculous department store."

"I tried to save the homes here," my father said, "but they're not safe. No one should live in these conditions. That's why I had new housing built in the suburbs just outside the city. It's beautiful there and you'll have a better quality of life."

"I'm homeless!" the stranger yelled.

He pulled out a gun, and my mother gasped in horror before pulling me further away with her.

"I gave you better homes. And transportation. And when the store is built, it'll provide hundreds of jobs. I did what I could to give back to my old community."

"You destroyed the community! You ruined everything!" He waved the gun as he yelled. "M-my entire life was here. And everyone left! They left me for grass and trees. But I'll never leave! You can't make me!"

I heard a loud pop. "Charlotte!" My father yelled as my mother screamed and covered me, holding me tightly against her as she whispered "Everything will be okay" over and over.

"N-n-no! Wh-what did I? I-I didn't mean--" The drunk wailed.

"It's okay," my dad said, and I felt relieved hearing his voice. "Just go and leave us be. I promise nothing will happen. I won't say a word."

I couldn't see anything with my mother holding me so tight. I heard someone stumble and the soft leather of a shoe slide against the sidewalk. I knew my father had collapsed. My mother sobbed.

"I--I have to finish this. It has to end here," the man murmured.

Suddenly there was another pop. Then one even closer before my mother slumped on top of me. I heard sirens and someone running. The stench of sweat and cheap alcohol still hung in the air.

"Bill!" Stewart's voice came from out of nowhere, then it was followed by a succession of pops that sounded different from the drunk's gun.

Stewart lifted my mother from me and gently laid her on her back on the cold cement. An intense iron smell filled the air. I couldn't grasp what happened.

"Will! Are you okay?" Stewart asked.

"Mom?" I choked as I nodded.

"She's alive."

"Dad?"

Stewart turned and I followed his eyes. My father laid in a black puddle I knew was his blood. Just beyond him was the body of the man with the gun. His head lay in a similar pool as my father's. I knew Stewart had killed him.

Hearing my father groan, I ran over. His hand clutched at his chest. His face was covered in sweat.

"Dad, are you ok?"

"I'm fine," he whispered and grasped my hand. "Take care of your mother. I'm sorry--" He coughed and spit up some blood. "I should've been more careful. I know better. But I wanted to show you the future." His breath grew ragged. "You and your mom are the best thing that ever happened to me."

I didn't hear the police and ambulances arrive. Several EMTs rushed over to my father and began working as my father's hand slowly let go of mine. I looked over at my mother who was now on a stretcher but not moving, her eyes still closed.

One of the EMTs working on my father put his hand on my shoulder and said "I'm sorry" in a strange accent.

Rushing over to my mother, Stewart stood beside her, listening to that technician.

"It doesn't look good. We have to get her to the hospital and operate. I'm not sure if she'll survive the ride though."

Hot tears streamed down my face. I felt lost. This had to be a bad dream. My mother's eyes fluttered and I reached for her hand. She quickly squeezed it, but there was no other sign she knew I was there.

As I climbed into the ambulance with her, the steady beep of the machine changed to a high constant hum. No one needed to say anything. I had lost them both.

Present Day

Clearing my throat, I composed myself again. Thinking about their deaths made me experience it all over again. Switching my focus to Deborah made me smile. I only wished she knew how special and talented she really was.

Yes, I should have told her I owned Hargrove's, but I had nothing to do with the Annual Designer Challenge other than creating it in honor of my mother years ago. Had I known Deborah would get so upset, I would've done things differently.

Still, she overreacted. Once we got to France and she saw the surprises I had for her, I was sure all of this ridiculousness would be forgotten.

Chapter Thirteen

Deborah

Why couldn't he have sat at the back of the plane? Sitting on the oversized leather plane seat, it didn't matter how angry and hurt I was, every time I looked up, I saw the back of Will's stupid head and my anger subsided a little bit. He really didn't do anything wrong, but he still should have told me. Now I needed a way out of showing my collection.

No way was I going to embarrass myself. I could just hear the whispers--*well, what do you expect, she's screwing the owner*. That was the last way I wanted to make a name for myself in the fashion industry.

This had to be the longest plane ride on the planet. I thought it was going to be bad before because of my excitement, now it was worse because I had no reason to be excited. I was a fraud now, before I had talent.

Sighing, I pulled out the pad of paper I always carried with me and started sketching some ideas. I'd have to call the Hargrove buyer Amanda when I got to Paris, and I was sure she'd fire me on the spot. Maybe I should just let Will take care of it. It was his fault anyway.

I peeked at the front of the plane again. His dark brown hair looked even richer against the tan leather seat. It was official--I was crazy about him. I was still upset though.

***

We rode together in the limo to the Hotel Plaza Athenee in silence. Will wouldn't even look at me, which was fine because if he did, I might want to kiss him. Besides, I really didn't want to look at him, either. Looking at him made it harder to stay angry with him for ruining my career.

But did he ruin my career? Was I being dramatic and blowing things out of proportion? Probably, but I couldn't change how I felt or my reaction. There was nothing worse in my mind than getting so close to achieving a dream, only to find out you achieved nothing.

Paris was more beautiful than I ever imagined. I wondered if I would get time to tour some spots or if Hargrove's would send me back immediately. Will certainly wasn't saying anything, but he didn't know I couldn't show my collection.

As we pulled up in front of the hotel, I marveled at how pretty a building could look. With cascading flowers tumbling from window boxes and red awnings, the exterior was lovely enough. Noticing the curved stone of the balconies, the intricately carved window accents, and the scalloped awning above the entrance simply took my breath away.

"Follow me," Will growled in my direction as we exited the limo.

Stewart directed the bellhop with our luggage while I followed Will like a puppy through the revolving doors and into the lobby. So in awe of everything around me, it never occurred to me to question anything.

The marble Art Deco lobby was framed by columns and large crystal chandeliers. Each of the columns had a vase with an arrangement of white orchid sprays. We walked through the lobby and directly to a small elevator without stopping.

"You two go up. I'll ride with the bellhop and your bags," Stewart said.

Will and I got onto the elevator and stood apart. I couldn't take it any longer. I had to say something.

"Are you going to say something?"

"You've made your feelings known. What more is there to say?" he said callously.

"There's plenty to say!" I said angrily. "Like how about sorry? Did you ever think of that?"

"I have nothing to apologize for."

"You know how hard I worked for that competition. No one else will realize that or care. All they're going to see is that I was your girlfriend."

"Was?" he roared as he finally looked at me.

Shaking his head, he stepped out of the elevator as soon as it opened and began walking down the hall. I quickly followed him, trying to keep up with his long stride, not knowing what else to say but wanting to fight some more. Opening the door to a room, he stepped back and handed the key to me.

"Your suite," he growled, then walked down the hall and disappeared into another room.

Squeezing the key in my hand, I shook it, pretending it was a mini-Will. Why was he being such a jerk?! How did he think I'd react when I found out my designs didn't win on their own? I should've known better than to think I was talented enough to show a collection at Fashion Week.

Entering the room, I was taken aback by the view out of the huge windows of the Eiffel Tower. Like the rest of the hotel, the suite was also fitted in the Art Deco style. The main room was decorated in cool light blues and tans. I had never been in a hotel room that had more than a couple of beds covered in polyester. Out of the corner of my eye, I spotted something red on the floor leading to one of the doors. The red stood out and seemed out of place on the dark wood floor. Will must have paid a lot of money for this place, there was no reason why it shouldn't be perfect. As I picked up the phone to call room service and let them know they left a mess in my suite, it slowly dawned on me that those were rose petals.

"Oh crap! I really did it this time," I said, realizing everything Will had done for me.

I followed them into the bedroom where they ended in a large heart on the cream-colored bedding of the king-sized bed. At the other end of the bedroom, I noticed the largest bouquet of red roses on a table, and just beyond it was a view of the Eiffel Tower again.

Tears rolled down my cheeks as I realized what a jerk I had been, not him. Sure, I was still hurt and upset, but I definitely overreacted.

The phone made a double-ring sound that startled me out of my pity party. Running to grab it, I hoped it was Will.

"Hello?"

"I have a message for Miss Deborah Hansen," said the hotel operator.

"Yes?" *Please be from Will, please be from Will.*

"Miss Dianna Brubaker said to tell you she was catching a red eye and should be here this afternoon."

"Oh, thank you." I couldn't help but feel disappointed. "Wait, are you still there?"

"Yes, Miss."

"Can you tell me what room Mr. William King is staying in?"

"No, I'm sorry, I don't have the specifics, but I can tell you that your room is connected to another suite and a deluxe guest-room."

Realizing there was a locked door in the bedroom, I wondered if Will was on the other end. "Thank you for your help," I said into the phone.

"My pleasure, Miss."

Chewing on my lip, I walked up to the door. *Could he be in there?* I pressed my ear up against the door and thought I heard something, and my heart almost leapt out of my chest. *It has to be him!*

I knocked softly and waited, but nothing happened. Knocking a little louder, I held my breath as I heard shuffling on the other side of the door. The handle turned and I stepped back as the door slowly opened. Dianna peeked around from behind the door.

"Dammit, Dianna!" I said, then immediately felt bad. "I mean hi, sorry."

"Well, hello to you too," she said as she stepped into my room. "I just got in, how did you know I was here? My plane was early."

"I didn't. I was hoping you were Will."

"Will? You mean Mr. Sexy came with you? What did the big boss man have to say about that?"

"They're the same person." I said then sighed, realizing how much had happened in the past day.

"You mean Will owns Hargrove's? But I thought it was a family owned store. That's not his last name. That explains why he looked familiar though."

"Hargrove is a family name. What do you mean that explains why he looked familiar?"

"His portrait is probably up on the top floor. You know, where they interviewed you for the contest," she said as she stared out at the view.

"Are you kidding me? Am I that blind?"

I thought back and remembered Will telling me to call him by his name and how surprised he seemed that I didn't recognize him. How could I not notice his picture?

"You should see my room! It's gorgeous," she said as she looked around my suite. "Ok, it's a little smaller than yours but still, isn't this place amazing?"

"Yeah, fabulous," I said unenthusiastically.

"What's wrong? You're in the City of Love with a gorgeous billionaire. If you have a problem with that, I'd be more than willing to fill in for you.

Just look at those roses! And the petals on the bed are a nice touch. He is getting lucky tonight!"

"No, he's not. We broke up."

"What are you talking about? You couldn't have done more than fly together. What happened?"

"Dianna, he owns Hargrove's. I just won the Designer Challenge. I can't show at Fashion Week now. It was rigged. I'll just be nothing more than the owner's girlfriend."

"Did he say that? Because last I knew, you didn't even know he was the owner, so why would anyone even know he had a girlfriend? Or even care?"

"He's the owner, of course it was rigged. And it does matter! I'm not good enough to have my own collection on display, and this proves it."

"No Deb, he's the owner. Do you think he even has time to bother with something as insignificant as a contest? And I saw your collection. It's gorgeous! Look at it yourself if you don't want to believe me."

Dianna looked around the bedroom and when she didn't see what she searched for, she went into the main room of my suite. Not knowing what to expect, I followed her and was surprised to see my bags sitting beside the door. Placing my old hard-sided suitcase on the couch, she opened it up and one by one pulled out the pieces of my collection, ending with the ocean blue gown.

"Look at these! How can you say these aren't worthy of winning?"

"You're right, they're good, but are they good enough? We're not just talking about Hargrove's but Fashion Week in Paris!"

"Then make something new. Add something to the collection to prove to yourself how good you really are."

"Are you crazy? There's no time!"

"Give me a break Deborah, I know you. I've seen how you sketch whenever you get a new idea. I bet you have new sketches already, and I also bet that if we go out right now, something will spark your imagination."

"You're right. And you can't go to Paris and not visit the Eiffel Tower. I mean, look at it out there." I looked out the window again and noticed the sun had begun its descent. "Let's go for a walk. Plus if we don't go tonight, I'm not sure if we'll get the time to before we go."

Dianna and I grabbed our handbags and left the hotel. With the sun almost beyond the horizon, a deep orange haze glowed just above the skyline as the Eiffel Tower beckoned us with its lights. We walked quietly at first, just taking in the scenery, until I spotted her slyly looking over at me a couple of times.

"Okay, what is it?" I asked.

"I have to know. Are you going to show your collection?"

"I think I am. I mean, my collection is really strong and I'm proud of it. I did win the contest after all. You're right, Will's got better things to do than to rig a contest. I don't know what I was thinking."

"I'm glad. You really do deserve it. I've been working at Hargrove's for a few years now and I've never seen a collection as good as yours. I even tried one year, but my designs just...well, they sucked," she said, laughing. "I made it to the interview before they promptly laughed me back onto the sales floor."

"That's terrible, Dianna!"

"No, it's really fine. I have no regrets. It was just something I really wanted to try, but I'm really not creative enough. Not like you."

As we walked past the squared trees lining the Champs de Mars, I began to lose myself in our surroundings. The Eiffel Tower made me think of modern mesh fabric. As I looked at its shape, I suddenly thought of an A-line dress. Just simple and elegant like the building in front of us.

"Oh wait, wait!" I said to Dianna.

Moving aside to let the other walkers pass, I pulled a notepad and pencil out of my bag. Frantically, I began sketching a sleeveless, form-fitting dress that easily went from day to night. As the dress followed the A shape, a softly ruffled hem finished the dress at mid-thigh.

"That's gorgeous! See what I mean, Deb? That's talent right there. I can even see how the Eiffel Tower inspired that dress."

"Thanks! We have to head back. I think I have some ivory crepe that will be perfect for this dress. I want to make the pattern tonight. Maybe they'll even let me send it down the runway!"

Excited didn't begin to explain how I felt. I loved this new dress and I had to make it a reality. I felt my confidence coming back and wondered how I let it slip away so easily. Briefly, I thought I should apologize to Will for overreacting, but the thought zipped out of my mind as quickly as it entered. All I could think about was creating that dress.

Chapter Fourteen

Deborah

I spent most of the night creating a pattern for the new dress and then cutting the fabric. It was the quickest I had ever designed anything and I couldn't believe how much I loved it.

Out of the corner of my eye, the sun began to rise. I kept the curtains open so I could look out at my inspiration as I worked on the dress. I couldn't have made the progress I did without seeing it right there. The view from the suite was perfect.

I couldn't wait to tell Will about the new dress and how inspired I got. That was until I realized he thought we had broken up. How could I forget that? What if he didn't want to talk to me? Or worse, what if he flew back home? He didn't even know how I really felt about him.

A soft knock on the door pulled me out of my funk. I knew it was Dianna. That meant it was time for us to head over to the Carrousel du Louvre where all Fashion Week activities would take place.

"Have you been working all night?" Dianna asked.

"Yes, and I really think it's perfect," I said as I pulled the dress onto a dress form. "I just need to do some minor adjustments, but most of those will come during the fitting anyway. Are you ready to go?"

"You have no idea how much I'm looking forward to this. How many people can say they worked on a collection at Fashion Week? Don't answer that, you'll ruin it for me."

"I packed up everything else already. I know you need your morning coffee, so we can ask the concierge for a place to stop at on our way."

"Sounds good. I'm ready to have some café au lait, just saying it sounds special. Have you spoken to Will?"

I didn't want to answer her. Feeling foolish, I tried to think of a quick change of topic but drew a blank. Instead, as I packed up the new dress, I shook my head, hoping she'd drop it.

"You said the front desk told you there are three rooms attached together. Why didn't you knock on the last door?"

"I got so wrapped up in designing this and having it ready on time, I completely forgot they said that. Plus it's not like I'm going to knock on the door in the middle of the night. What if it's not even him?"

She rolled her eyes, making it clear she wasn't falling for my bullshit. Ignoring her, I finished packing up the things I needed for the fittings.

"Why are you doing this?" she asked. "I mean, there's a gorgeous man who came all the way out here with you and you're ignoring him! Sure, you're busy and all, but the last thing he probably remembers is you yelling at him. I know how upset you were when I got here. I can only imagine how you acted towards him when you found out."

"Okay, you're right! Happy? I'm an idiot and honestly I'm too embarrassed by how I acted to see him. Do you have any idea how I felt when I saw that heart made of rose petals on the bed? I mean seriously, who does that? I don't deserve him."

"You *are* an idiot, Deborah. And if you really think fate didn't bring you two together, then you're a bigger moron than I thought. I saw how he looks at you. It's like nothing in the world even exists but you. You can manage a few minutes to make sure things are okay between the two of you."

I sighed, knowing she was right. I needed to talk to Will and I might as well do it now before things got too crazy with Fashion Week. Who knew what Will thought of me now or if he even thought of me at all? He seemed really angry when he left me in the hall, but I didn't want to lose him because of my own stupidity.

Putting my ear to the other hotel room door in the main living space of my suite, I listened like I did at Dianna's door but didn't hear anything. *Did he leave? Is he staying somewhere else?* It was early, so maybe he was still asleep. I shouldn't bother him.

As I stepped away from the door, Dianna entered the room with her arms folded tightly over her chest. She didn't need to say anything for me to know what she thought. I was chickening out.

Taking a deep breath, I gathered my courage then softly knocked on the door and waited a second before giving up. Dianna let out an annoyed sigh, reached around me, and knocked loudly before walking away. I was just about to run after her when the door opened.

"I'm busy," Will said as he let go of the door and re-entered his room.

Following him, I immediately felt bad. Will chose to stay in an ordinary guest room while Dianna and I had spacious, luxurious suites. Even in his anger towards me, he let me enjoy the posh finery and the view.

Wearing a black suit, Will walked back and forth through the room as he packed things into his suitcase. Slowly it dawned on me what was going on.

"What are you doing?" I asked him as I looked into his suitcase. "Where are you going?"

"I'm going home," he said between clenched teeth.

"No, you can't leave."

"I have no interest in fashion and unless you've changed your mind, Hargrove's doesn't have a collection to present. I have no reason to stay." He was quiet while he continued packing then looked at me. The green flecks in his eyes flashed angrily then softened. "I'm sorry. I should have told you exactly who I was. I liked that you weren't into me because of Hargrove's, and I didn't tell you because I didn't want to risk things changing."

"I was wrong," I whispered.

"What?"

"I was wrong," I said quietly.

"Speak up, I can't hear you."

I cleared my throat and finally spoke at a normal volume. "I was wrong."

"What was that?" he said as he turned away with his crooked grin.

"You jerk! You heard me."

"And?"

"And I'm sorry I made such a big deal over something stupid. But you have to see it from my side."

"I do understand, Deborah. I know your concerns are valid, but I really have nothing to do with the Designer Challenge. I was just as surprised when I found out you won and immediately wanted to surprise you with this trip."

"Dianna helped talk some sense into me. I even designed an amazing new dress that I added to the collection."

"I'm glad. You really do deserve this opportunity. And since we're up a little early, why don't we go for a drive today? Just you and me."

"Just the two of us?"

"Yes. It's morning, so there's plenty of time. Let's drive out to the countryside. I hear it's beautiful."

"I don't know, Will. I'm supposed to do measurements today. The next time I see the models, I'll be dressing them for the runway. Let me meet the models and see what I can do. In the meantime, bring your bags to my room."

Standing on tiptoes, I reached up, pulled him down to me, and kissed him. All was right in the world again.

Chapter Fifteen

Deborah

As the taxi arrived at the Louvre, the first thing I noticed was the glass pyramid, which looked even more impressive than in photos. Dianna and I peeled ourselves off the windows as we soaked in as much of Paris as we could during the ride. Expecting a long day on my feet, I dressed comfortably in a pair of tan linen cropped pants with a black floral print empire waist top.

Apparently all this time there were cocoons in my stomach just waiting for me to arrive at the *Carrousel du Louvre,* because as soon as I got out of the taxi, hundreds of butterflies filled my stomach.

Entering the mall that hosted Fashion Week, we were in awe as we walked along the gleaming ivory marble floors, not much different than those at work, but somehow much more glamorous to us.

Following the flow of people wearing some of the most eclectic styles, I felt a little plain being dressed so casually but knew I was finally where I dreamed of being.

While the show didn't start for another couple of days, today was really important because it was the first time we would meet our models and the last time we would see them until an hour before show time. The measurements we got today needed to be perfect.

Even everyone with their black glossy Fashion Week access passes dangling around their necks seemed special. After collecting our passes, I looked at mine for a moment and smiled at seeing 'Deborah Hansen, Designer' printed across it.

A short red-haired woman with 'volunteer' on her badge showed us the space Hargrove's arranged for us to use for fittings and alterations. It was a white room with just enough room for two sewing machines, several dress forms, a long table, and a three-way mirror that reminded me of Will the day I took his measurements.

My palms were moist as I unpacked my designs and waited for the models to arrive. I had a lot of work ahead of me since I designed the clothes for a bigger girl than what the models would be.

"Look," Dianna said as she elbowed me, "the Amazons have arrived."

Stifling a giggle, I looked at the doorway. A group of ten tall, overly thin women walked into the room chatting with each other. My eyes darted quickly over their bodies as the butterflies in my stomach morphed into a twisted knot.

"Oh no, it's even worse than I imagined," I said under my breath.

All I could see were protruding collarbones, sunken cheeks, and clothes that hung off bodies no different than a plastic hanger. The models looked unhealthy. Some of the problems I saw could be fixed with hair and make-up, but the part that mattered to me the most was their bodies, and these models were much too thin.

"Are you okay?" Dianna asked quietly. "You look a little green."

Breathing deeply as I tried to calm myself, I opened my mouth to speak but squeaked instead. My throat felt like one of the models got lodged in there. Tears slowly stung my eyes so I looked around, trying to stop them from spilling onto my cheeks.

As I blinked and fought back tears, Will walked through the door with Stewart close behind him. *Don't let him see me like this!* Turning away, I hoped to somehow disappear or blend into the wall. It didn't work.

"I see your models have arrived," he said as he approached then lowered his head to my ear. "Did something happen? Is everything okay?"

The dam burst. "They're too skinny," I said, then covered my face with my hands.

"Yes well, they're models. Someone thinks they should look like the walking dead. You knew they'd be thin. I don't understand what's wrong."

"Everything! My designs are ruined. I'll have to start over. I can use my sketches, but I have two days to make everything over again."

"You can't use what you have?"

I shook my head. Just by looking at them, I could tell all my samples were a waste. Every detail, from the ruching to the draping, would have to be completely redone. My samples were worthless now. With that amount of work, it would be easier to start from scratch. The biggest problem was I didn't have time. It was close to impossible to recreate all of my designs in less than two days.

Will stormed off without a word and barked something at one of the models that sent her running off in tears. While he glared at her abandoned friend, she said something to him before she also left.

In the blink of an eye, an elegant older woman with 'Mimi' on the access pass hanging around her neck entered and began talking to Will. Based on the way she carried herself, she might have been a model back in the day. Will's voice boomed throughout the room as he spoke, this time in French. I wasn't sure if I should be worried or impressed that he could yell in another language.

With her face red, she barked something at the eight remaining models and they began filing out into the hall. With a quick turn on her heel, she exited the room and my dream went from impossible to non-existent. The sickly toothpick models were bad, but no models were worse. How would my collection go down the runway without them?

Not wanting to be there any longer than I needed to be, I started packing up. Will spoke in hushed angry tones to Stewart before coming back to me.

"What are you doing?" he asked

"What's it look like? I'm packing."

"Don't."

He crossed the room and exited. I hated feeling like such a wuss and knew some of it was from the lack of sleep, but all I wanted to do was feel sorry for myself. Poor me! I made my dream come true and was standing at Paris Fashion Week. Yeah, that pity party didn't last long.

My mind started to work, and I wondered how many women walking around the mall on the other level would walk down the runway for me. It couldn't hurt to ask.

"Let's go find some models, Dianna."

As we entered the hall, Mimi walked towards us with Will by her side. She reached out and held my hand between her cold bony hands as she spoke with a thick French accent.

"There was a horrible mistake. Gianni was supposed to be in this room, but he changed last minute. I've sent the girls to him, and yours should arrive soon."

She patted my hand when she finished talking and then shot Will an annoyed look before walking off. Dianna and I went back into the Hargrove's room and as I unpacked the few things I put away, my new models entered.

Now these were the real Amazons. My new models didn't look like they'd need to seek shelter on a windy day. They were as close to being normal women as one would find on the runway. These were the models used in plus sized ads, and while that made them controversial for runway, I couldn't be happier seeing them.

Breathing a sigh of relief, I held myself back from hugging Will, not wanting to reveal our relationship to all the strangers in the room. Dianna immediately got to work, taking measurements and a photo of each model. She came up with the idea that if we planned hair and make-up ahead of time, it would take the stress out of choosing their look after they were dressed. I loved the idea and couldn't wait until later when I'd play paper dolls with their photos.

As I pulled the measuring tape out of my sewing case, Will came up behind me and kissed my neck, sending goose bumps over my body. *So much for not revealing our relationship.* Truth was I didn't care anymore. People could say what they wanted. My designs deserved to be there.

"Mmm, you smell like oranges. Let's get out of here, just the two of us," he whispered before nibbling on my ear.

"We can't. I have a lot of work to get started on, and you know Stewart won't let you out of his sight."

"Look at Stewart. I think he's in love."

I scanned the crowded room a couple of times looking for him. He had an uncanny way of changing his appearance just with his body language, and for a brief moment I didn't recognize him. It wasn't until I realized Stewart was the man commanding the attention of two brunette models that I realized where he was.

"So? He's still not going to let you go alone."

"He doesn't need to know I'm going. I arranged for a 1959 BMW 507 to be delivered. It's a roadster, a two-seater. It's probably already outside. We can sneak out and tour the countryside."

"I'd love to, Will, really I would, but I need to be here. I can't just leave all this on Dianna."

"She won't mind. Look at her, she's loving this. Just ask her, okay? That's all I ask."

Dianna was busy taking measurements of a blonde model I recognized from a Vogue photo spread. I motioned to her that I wanted to talk and then stayed out of her way until she was done. She grinned happily as she walked over.

"Do you have any idea how awesome this is?" she asked. "Of course you do, you're here too, duh. I'm just so star struck right now, you have no idea."

"I know! Did you see some of the designers here? It's mind blowing to think I'm showing my collection on the same runway."

"You know," she said as she glanced over to Will, "if you want to go sightseeing with Mr. Sexy, you can."

"Where'd that come from?"

"I'm just saying that if the gorgeous man of my dreams was in the most romantic city in the world with me, I'd want to spend some quality time with him."

"I can't, Dianna. I can't leave you here alone to work while I run off and have fun. It's not right."

"No, you have to. I'll never have an experience like this again, and I know you will. While you're gone, I'm not going to lie, I'm going to pretend it's my collection," she said as she laughed. "Plus I need to live vicariously through you, remember? If you don't spend some alone time with Will, then I won't have anything to dream about. I will be expecting details in the morning when we get to work on the alterations and everything else."

"Are you sure? I really do feel bad..."

"Go! We're done talking about it. I have models to measure dahling, now shoo!" she said with a snooty fake accent.

Dianna gently pushed me away as I wondered what I did to deserve such a great friend. Will looked at me anxiously as I returned.

"Well? What did she say?"

"She told me to go. And Stewart?"

"Smitten. It's nice to see him enjoying himself for once. Now let's go before we lose our chance."

He grabbed my hand and led me to the back of the room. Behind the three-way mirror was a door I hadn't noticed before. It opened to a long marble hallway that we followed until we reached the entrance with the crystal triangle.

"Good, I see the car arrived," Will said as he looked ahead towards the antique shiny red roadster.

"And what's so special about this car?" I asked as we approached it.

"Everything. Limited run, almost made BMW go bankrupt, Elvis owned one, I could go on and on."

The convertible was gorgeous and didn't look its age, but until I noticed Will couldn't stop grinning as he got into the car, I didn't realize the significance of it. He had never had his own car before. For his entire life, Stewart had driven him wherever he needed to go.

"Where are we going?"

"Remember the gate in front of King Manor?"

"The one your mom told you stories about?"

"That one. I found the monastery and I've always wanted to see it."

"Then let's go!"

As Will steered the car out of the city, I enjoyed the warm sunshine and the wind blowing through my hair. We drove out of the city in silence as we soaked in the beauty of the city. The architecture was a combination of the old, with Greek and Gothic influences, and the new. Somehow the city joined old and new together like a complex jazz piece with all the instruments working together to create music.

The further away from Paris we got, the more open the landscape was. Eventually we were surrounded by green rolling hills that reminded me of the landscape of Canyon Cove. If it wasn't for the occasional spire of a centuries-old church or the cut of a castle against the sky, the two places might have been interchangeable.

After about an hour into the drive, Will reached for his folded suit jacket, pulled a folded map out of the inside pocket, and placed it on my lap.

"I need your help. We should be right around here," he said as he tapped a yellow section of the map. "I circled the monastery in red, let me know where I need to turn. I think it's coming up and I was told it's hard to spot from the road."

As I collected my bearings looking at the map, I found the turn off he was talking about and placed my finger on it. "Wait, you asked about the monastery? Don't you think Stewart will find out? Knowing him, he'll be there waiting for us."

Will laughed. "No, he's not going to care."

"I think you're forgetting who you're talking about. He seems very concerned about you being in danger."

Will's knuckles whitened on the hand that rested on the shift stick while his face grimaced. Thinking I struck a nerve, I dropped it. The last thing I wanted to do was ruin a day out with him in such a romantic location. My big mouth messed things up enough for one trip.

"The road should be right up here," I said after spotting a mile marker the map indicated before the turn.

An old, stone-carved road marker had the name of our turn, and Will slowed down as he maneuvered the car onto the road. The dirt road was packed so tight from centuries of use that we didn't have to worry about dust flying into the car.

After driving further down the lonely road, the monastery appeared in the distance. The white limestone silhouette of the abbey jutted up into the sky, growing more luminescent as we arrived.

"How did your mom even find this place?"

"She loved history and this is one of the oldest monasteries," he said as we walked among the ruins. "You can see how the church still stands with its towers, and over there is what's left of the cloisters and the library. The original building is well over a thousand years old but was destroyed first by the Vikings, then later in wars after being rebuilt each time."

The abbey was the largest of the ruins and still impressive. It looked like a medieval castle, and I could easily imagine monks from centuries ago praying there. Following the path, we came upon two pylons on either side of where the path widened.

"This must've been where the gate was," he said as he walked over to one of the stone columns and placed his hand on it.

His face softened and briefly crumpled, and I knew he was thinking back on his brief childhood. It hurt to see how close to the surface those memories remained.

Hearing a sound come from the abbey, I turned around but saw nothing. *Probably just an animal,* I thought. As I looked up into Will's face, his eyes brightened, and he wrapped his arms around me.

"Thank you for coming here with me. You have no idea what this means to me," he said before kissing my forehead.

"Of course. I can't imagine being anywhere else."

"Well, isn't this sweet," a male voice with a thick Eastern European accent echoed against the ruins. "Come out, Marco. It's him."

As I turned around, I saw another man approaching from one of the other ruins. Marco was a monster of a man in a black t-shirt and a bald head. The man who spoke looked exactly the same except for his crooked nose, which must have been busted years ago. Will tightened his grip on me as they came closer, but it didn't matter.

Marco grabbed my arm and roughly pulled me out of Will's grasp while the man who spoke lifted a gun to Will's head. I couldn't breathe. I considered screaming but knew there was no one around to help. As I trembled in fear, Marco squeezed his thickly muscled arm like a boa constrictor around me further, as if to tell me I was in more danger than I realized.

"Oscar, what to do with the girl? Kill her now, yes? That will be fun," Marco said with a cheerfulness in his voice that sent chills down my spine.

"No, no. We bring her to Dimitri, too. She might be useful. At the very least, she might be helpful in making this one talk."

"We only have one injection."

"Use it on her," Oscar said, then slammed the blunt end of the gun into Will's temple.

"No! Will!" I screamed as his body collapsed to the ground. I felt a sharp prick at the base of my neck. My body went limp as I fought him. Using all my might, I tried to shove his enormous arm off me, but my limbs wouldn't move. Suddenly my vision blurred and Marco slung me over his shoulder. Hanging like a rag doll, everything spun before going black.

Chapter Sixteen

Will

Slowly lifting my head off my chest, I tried focusing my eyes. Seated on a wooden chair with my arms tied behind me, I closed my eyes and tried to push past the throbbing in my head.

I wasn't alone. Voices spilled into the room, bouncing off the stone walls moist with condensation. The grey flagstone floor chilled my bare feet as I wondered why they took me and where I was.

"Deborah?" I whispered, hoping she was close.

I'd never forgive myself if anything happened to her. Inhaling deeply, I caught the faint whiff of oranges. She had to be near.

I tried to move my arms, pushing against the ropes to loosen them, but nothing came of it other than my realizing my arms were tied to more than just my chair. Moving and stretching my hands as much as I could, I finally felt the soft flesh of her hand with my fingertips.

"Will..." she whispered, her words slurring, "please be you."

"Yes, it's me."

"They drugged me...I...I..."

"Shhh, don't speak. I'll get us out of here somehow."

The only light in the windowless room came from a single bulb dangling from the ceiling. Voices echoed against the stone from an adjoining room. Forcing myself to focus despite the pain in my head, I was able to make out a long metal table and a few chairs.

Attempting to use my legs as leverage, I realized my ankles were tied to the chair. Pushing with my feet, our chairs scraped along the stone floor. Not wanting to draw attention, I stopped as my mind spun.

It was useless to struggle. Whoever these men were wanted us there. They knew what they were doing. Hearing a soft sob behind me, I flexed and struggled against the ropes to get enough leeway to reach her hand, which quickly closed around mine.

"What's going on? Who are these people?" she cried, her voice filled with fear.

"I wish I knew," I said as a tall, thick-bodied silhouette filled the doorway.

A man in a tight black t-shirt and shaved head nodded towards us. "Dimitri, they're up," he announced with a thick indescribable accent.

"It's about time. I was worried you killed another one too soon with that stuff," Dimitri joked.

Dimitri's accent was American, but there was something else underneath it. As he stepped towards the light, I was surprised to see he was a slender built man with closely cropped black hair. His looks weren't remarkable or startling like his companions. Dimitri could easily blend in with a crowd. In a lot of ways, he reminded me of Stewart.

The two men entered the small space where Deborah and I were tied up. The giant man's face was expressionless but more calming than Dimitri's eerie grin.

"Let the girl go, you don't need her," I said, knowing they only wanted me and hoping to get Deborah to safety.

"William Hargrove King, the Third," Dimitri said slowly as he stepped directly in front of me. "You are correct. We don't want her. But we don't even want you. Make this easy, tell us where your father is, and you can both walk out of here."

"My father? If you're asking where he is, then you're even dumber than I thought. He's dead."

"Wrong," he said as a strong hand struck my cheek.

The force of his hand was enough to move our chairs back. As my cheek stung then burned, I glared at him.

His eyes narrowed intensely as he looked down at me. "I don't have time to play around, William. Again, where is your father?"

"In a fucking cemetery. Where he's been most of my life."

I didn't know what happened. In an instant, I felt pain quickly spread across my face and down my neck. He must've punched me, but his fist flew so fast I didn't see it. The chair held me so tight, the force of his knuckles jerked my head back and into Deborah's as the chairs jerked back. If our chairs hadn't been connected, Dimitri's punch would have knocked me over.

"I don't have the patience for this. I'm only asking you one more time before I get the poker. Trust me, you don't want that. Where is your father?"

Meeting his stare as the blood trickled from my nose, I could see he wanted an answer I wasn't able to give. I didn't know how to convince him of my father's death. Did this asshole really think he was alive?

"He's in the St. James Cemetery. With my mother," I said through clenched teeth. "Now let us go!"

My voice echoed throughout the room. Dimitri's goon cracked a smile before walking out.

"That's what he wants people to think, but I know better. He's still active. I recognized his work. He stole from the wrong man."

"What are you talking about? He was murdered. I saw him die!" I yelled angrily.

"A man like that doesn't die so easily. I know the kind of man your father is. He wouldn't leave his son orphaned and ignorant," he said as he paced in front of me.

Carefully carrying a rusted iron fire poker, its pointed tip glowing red from the heat, Dimitri's goon almost looked giddy. I still had no idea who these men were or why they kept asking for my dead father, but it was clear they meant business.

"Maybe this will jog your memory," Dimitri said as he took the hot poker from his assistant and admired its red tip.

Deborah sobbed from behind me, and I was glad she couldn't see what was going on. I thought back to that fateful night of my parents' murder and realized not seeing might be worse. I wanted to comfort her.

"Everything will be okay," I whispered.

Squeezing her hand the best I could, I felt her squeeze back just before Dimitri swung the tip of the hot poker into my shoulder.

A searing pain shot through my arm and into my neck, forcing me to let go of Deborah's hand. Clenching my teeth, I growled in agony. The smell of burning cotton and flesh filled the air.

I felt the heat of my blood ooze from the wound as my sleeve became soaked and stuck against my skin. Deborah twisted in her seat, trying to see what happened.

"Fuck you!" I said between clenched teeth before lowering my voice. "I'm okay, Deborah. It's just...my shoulder...a fireplace poker..."

The room swayed between the pain in my shoulder and the throbbing still in my head. The light went out as a gust of wind entered the room, leaving us in total darkness. I squeezed Deborah's hand reassuringly although I didn't know what was going on.

"Everything will be okay," I whispered.

The sounds of confused men echoed against the stone walls from the other room. As I tried to force my eyes to adjust, the only thing I could see was a thin line of light seeping through a boarded-up window I hadn't noticed before.

"Stay put."

The commanding male voice was familiar. I straightened, frozen as my mind tried to make sense of it. All the pain was replaced by confusion.

"It can't be," I whispered.

"Who?" Deborah asked, her voice hoarse.

I didn't answer her. I couldn't. I had to be wrong. I hadn't heard that voice in twenty-five years.

The clank of the fire poker hitting the floor filled the room, followed by the smell of iron I recognized as blood. Shouts came from the other room but were quickly silenced. I thought I heard the unmistakable heavy boots of the large man running but then nothing. Only deafening silence.

The dangling light bulb switched on, momentarily blinding me as it swung back and forth. Once my eyes adjusted, I spotted Dimitri lying face down on the floor, the poker sticking through his chest, propping him up slightly off the floor as he lay in a black pool of his own blood.

Just beyond him was his giant assistant, sprawled out on the floor like a mountain. That was enough for me. I turned as much as I could to check on Deborah and realized the rope around us had been loosened.

Quickly slipping out of our ties, we clutched at each other, glad to be free. Deborah pushed away and gently touched my wounded shoulder, making me wince.

"It'll be fine, let's just get out of here," I said as I looked around, unsure which way to go.

"This way," Stewart said from the doorway as he wiped his hands, his forceful voice surprising me.

Grabbing Deborah's hand, I could tell she wasn't steady on her feet. I slipped my arm underneath hers and helped her towards Stewart into the adjoining room. We stepped over several men dressed similar to our kidnappers earlier with their dark t-shirts and bald heads. I recognized Stewart's work in there from the last attempt on my life. But who was in the room with us?

Without a word, we followed Stewart outside where a car waited, its engine already running. He opened the back door and I helped Deborah inside. The fresh air seemed to help diffuse the effects of the drug, and she smiled softly at me.

I held her, my arms wrapped around her soft comforting body, her head against my uninjured shoulder, as Stewart drove. It wasn't long before I realized he was heading towards the ruins of the monastery and not Paris.

"Stewart? Why are we going back to the monastery?"

"There's unfinished business."

I didn't question him. Stewart had saved my life countless times. He raised me. There was no reason to question him. He wouldn't answer anyway.

As he parked the car beside my roadster, I was glad to be back. The place made me feel close to my mother again and filled me with warmth.

With Stewart following, Deborah and I walked along the abbey, marveling once again at the enormity of the structure as we tried forgetting what we had just been through.

"Your mother really loved this place more than any other," said the voice from the darkened room.

Bracing myself for the only possibility, I turned around. He stood beside Stewart, shorter than I remembered and with more grey in his hair, but it was unmistakable. The man was my father.

"I haven't been back here since she passed," he said, sounding a little sad as he looked back at the abbey. "I always suspected Dimitri watched this place. Although that wasn't what kept me away."

"How?" I asked, stunned. "How are you still alive? And why didn't you tell me?"

"You couldn't know. Only Stewart knew, and he had been sworn to secrecy. I had to protect you from the men who were after me. Those men you met today."

"Protect me?! You're the reason I've lived in danger all these years." I yelled.

All the pain and anger from losing my parents so young came back. It was never buried very deep. Here was the man I idolized as a child, half of the world I lost all those years ago, back from the grave, and I couldn't help but wish he was still dead.

"She died because of you," I accused him. "I've blamed some stupid drunk all these years, but it really was because of you, wasn't it?"

"You're right, I should have known better. I was trained to know better. I got sloppy. I thought I was indestructible. I became too cocky and didn't realize the danger I put my family in."

"That's your excuse? You got sloppy? Fuck you, Dad! It wasn't just some mess, it was our life. I was a child! My parents were killed in front of me. Didn't you think about how that would affect me? And then you left Stewart to raise me instead of doing it yourself."

"Stewart's better than me," he said quietly. "I couldn't stay with you. I had to leave. Then they were after me. Stewart is smarter, quicker, more lethal than I ever was. You were safer with him."

"Bill, you owe Will an explanation. He deserves to know what happened," Stewart said. "Tell him the truth."

Everything I had seen of Stewart throughout the years suddenly clicked. All my suspicions about him, the things I thought were too absurd to be true, were confirmed. Stewart wasn't just a driver. He was a trained killer.

"You left your child in the hands of a killer," I said bitterly.

"You were safe! I did what I had to do. I never expected what happened that night to happen. That drunk--"

"I don't want to hear it," I interrupted.

I couldn't imagine telling him how much it hurt to see him. How his standing there, and my knowing he had been well for so many years, made the loss of my mother that much more of a tragedy, and I felt like I was losing her all over again.

Looking at Stewart, I realized how important to my life he really was. He had no obligation to stay with me, yet he did. It was more than I could say for my own father.

I had no more words. I couldn't look at the man who was my father anymore. I had to leave. Looking down at Deborah still in my arms, I slowly let go.

"I'm sorry," I said to her before storming off towards my car.

"Will, wait!" My father called after me, but I didn't care. He had been dead for the past twenty-five years. He could stay dead.

"Will!" Deborah cried out.

I felt bad leaving her, but I had to get out of there. I needed to get away from all the memories that haunted me for so many years. Stewart would take care of her. She was better off without me anyway.

Speeding back to Paris, I called and made a plane reservation, something I had never done before. I didn't want to be William Hargrove King, the Third in his private jet. I wanted to be as anonymous as possible. Besides, Stewart and Deborah needed the jet more than I did.

As I sat at the airport waiting for the plane to board, I spotted several small families similar to my own as a child. Tragedy in any form has an amazing way of changing the world for a person. I once was that innocent child and in a flash became something else.

The words I once considered to be my father's last rang through my head. *No regrets.* Such simple yet powerful words. But thinking about my father brought all my anger back, this time mixed with the pain of loss.

Even without the events with my father, this trip with Deborah had proven to be more complicated than I had planned. Things were simpler before when I was alone.

Chapter Seventeen

Deborah

"Will!" I cried out as he left.

Still not feeling like myself, I couldn't run after him. He didn't want to be chased anyway. My head swam as I tried to understand everything that happened. It felt like I was in a bad dream.

Will's father was expressionless. I couldn't understand how he could be so cold. He hadn't seen his son in all this time and all he had for him were excuses. I looked at the older version of Will standing before me and wondered why he hadn't left yet.

"What the hell is wrong with you?" I demanded as I glared at him. "That's your son! I don't understand everything that just happened, but I don't see how any parent could let their child walk away like that. How can you let him leave? You're abandoning him again!"

"You couldn't begin to understand," he said.

"Why don't you try me?"

I challenged his gaze as he stood quietly. He paced the grounds, looking like he had something to say. As I waited, he looked over at Stewart, who nodded.

"On one condition," Bill said. "You have to promise to tell Will my story. Maybe then he'll understand."

"Of course. He deserves to know."

Will's father looked up at the abbey wistfully. Lost in thought for a moment, he cracked his knuckles one by one. He spoke quietly at first.

"I guess the best place to start is the beginning," he said. "I am William Hargrove King, Jr. But most people call me Bill."

Chapter Eighteen
Bill

"As a boy growing up in poverty, I knew I didn't have many choices in my life. My parents tried as hard as they could to provide my brothers and I with what they could, but it was rare we could afford anything special or new.

"Still, the neighborhood was nowhere near as decrepit as the night I took Will to see his future, the flagship Hargrove's store. It's sad how that one tragic event formed the person he became.

"Back when I was a child, that section of Canyon Cove was mostly populated by immigrants. Will's grandparents came to the United States with very little in their pockets and nothing more than a dream to guide them.

"My father went by Will, too. The family called me Bill to minimize confusion. With all of his savings from working as a day laborer, my father was able to open the first Hargrove's store. He named it Hargrove's to honor his mother, my grandmother, whose name we carried.

"But my father's Hargrove's wasn't anything like the one in existence now. Instead of hundreds of fine department stores, my father's shop was a corner market where neighborhood folk could buy a few groceries and other basic items. I wanted a better life than that.

"During my last year of high school, an army recruiter came in and made an impressive presentation. He offered us exotic locales and training we could build on for the rest of our lives. I was sold. I didn't need any more specifics other than it was a way out of that tiny corner of Canyon Cove.

"After enlisting, I was required to take an exam to test my psyche. Somehow this multiple-choice test told them my best fit within the military. Needless to say, I look at things a bit differently than others and they determined my best fit was as a sniper.

"The recruiter didn't lie. I did get to travel, but I can't say any of the locales were particularly exotic. If anything, it made me appreciate the beauty of Canyon Cove more, and that is why when I decided to lay down roots, I moved back.

"Don't get me wrong, I was the first to admit I never wanted roots. Bill King didn't want to settle down, and my occupation made my loneliness practically a requirement. To be honest, I preferred my own company to that of others. At least until I met Charlotte, Will's mother. I remember it like it was yesterday."

Thirty-five Years Ago

The military didn't keep their killers for long. Something to do with dehumanization. So after I completed my four years, they offered me another position. It was their way of making sure their assassins didn't snap from overwork. It takes a special mindset to be able to continue this job successfully.

Retirement in my twenties was the furthest thing on my mind though. I loved my job and I was making more money than I knew what to do with. Since the military didn't want me anymore, I learned how to do it in the private sector by taking contracts.

I was down the Jersey Shore on an assignment when I first saw her. As I stood on the busy boardwalk, with its spin-the-wheel games and noisy rides, I pretended to be a tourist people-watching.

I even dressed the part. The best killers know how to blend into their environment. I wore a brown and tan striped cabana boy shirt with a pair of tan slacks and loafers, just like every other man my age.

The reason for this hit was a small crime syndicate. It had sprung up in the sleepy shore town of Point Pleasant, and the powers that be wanted it squashed. Usually my focus was solely on my mark, but as I scanned the crowd, I couldn't help but notice a beautiful brunette sitting at a red picnic table eating waffles and ice cream with complete abandon. I found it refreshing.

At that point, I was only tracking to get an idea of my target's habits. He could wait. The girl couldn't. She had her wavy hair pulled back into a loose ponytail and a red and white gingham dress I recognized as the uniform the waitresses wore at the local diner. Pulling out my binoculars, I admired her full round face, rosy cheeks, and eyes so blue they put the sky to shame. Other boys might have called her plump, but she looked perfect to me.

Growing up, my mother always told me to beware of the girls who didn't eat. She believed that if a person couldn't enjoy food, they couldn't enjoy life. From my experiences, I had to agree. Seeing this gorgeous creature eating this Shore food staple gave me a yearning for companionship I never had before.

The girl sat in an area with twenty glossy red picnic tables next to one of the larger food stands. It wouldn't have surprised me if someone thought painting was equal to cleaning. The stand had a gaudy red and white blinking sign in the shape of an arrow, and most of their offerings sat under heat lamps in the already sweltering humidity.

I noticed the stand didn't serve what the girl was eating and figured it was my in to talk to her. Carefully stepping between the sticky tables, the heat of the day rising from the cement ground, I approached her table.

"Hey there, good looking, whatcha got there?" I asked with my usual swagger.

"Get lost buddy, I'm not in the mood."

She didn't even look up at me. Her face closed off with an expression that told me to go to hell before she continued eating as if I wasn't there. For me, it was love at first sight.

"I'm sorry, miss. I didn't mean to be rude," I said, hoping to charm her socks off. "You see, I'm from out of town. Canyon Cove to be exact. Not sure if you've ever heard of it."

"Do I look like I care?" she interrupted. "Look, I just got off a double and came down here to watch the waves when those two assholes over there decided they thought it would be funny to throw their sodas at me. I don't need any bullshit from you too."

She stuffed her mouth with chocolate ice cream and a piece of the Belgian waffle that cradled the ice cream. I was so busy admiring her before that I didn't notice the soda stains on her uniform or how the front of her hair was still a little wet. As a comfort eater myself, I suddenly realized why she attacked her dessert the way she did.

I looked over in the direction she pointed and saw two men in their early twenties. One had red hair, freckles, and a pug nose, the other had slicked back, greasy black hair. They catcalled the pretty girls who walked past and called the others names or spit on them.

"Those two over there?" I asked her.

Her brow wrinkled as she looked up at me for the first time before nodding her head. "Yeah, that's them. I grew up with those creeps. Even played with them as kids..."

I didn't need to hear any more. Briskly walking towards them, I hopped over the wooden railing between the tables and the boardwalk where they were perched. I put my arms around both their shoulders and smiled.

"You see that girl over there?" I asked as I nodded in her direction. "You touch her or say another word to her again, and I swear it'll be your last."

"Yeah? What are you gonna do? I've never seen you here before. You're not even from around here," said the redhead.

"Let me give you a preview."

Elbowing the greasy guy in the gut, he doubled over and I gave his head a quick shove into my rising knee, easily breaking his nose. Next, my fist flew into Red's solar plexus, causing him to drop to his knees in agony.

Hopping the fence back over to the girl, she looked at me with awe and a smile that showed off her perfect teeth. I bowed to her as she began clapping.

"What did that feel like? Oh, I would've loved to just punch Jay or Donnie once like that. I bet it felt great!" she said.

I laughed. "It did. But only because of what they did to you. I know guys like that, and they'll never bother you again." I looked at her for a moment, taken by her beauty and how full of life she seemed. "I'm sorry I hit on you. I should've realized you were upset. Guess I have bad timing."

"Wait. You were hitting on me?"

"Of course. Look at you."

"Yeah, look at me. I'm a mess. I'm in this stupid uniform and I'm stuffing my face because I felt bad for myself," she said.

"All I see is how beautiful you are. My name is Bill, by the way."

"Nice to meet you. I'm Charlotte."

Present Day

"We were together ever since. The day I convinced Charlotte to marry me was one of the happiest days of my life. The other was when Will was born.

"She never knew what I really did. She was so trusting and innocent. I used my dad's old Hargrove's store as a front and kept funneling money into it so it would grow. Once Will was born though, I didn't want to do the contracts anymore. I wanted to be home and be a normal family.

"I figured I would do one more job. Something of my own choosing. I discovered a new money-laundering scheme being run by a bunch of novices. I heard they were coming into a large sum and I figured I could take them out, take the cash, and no one would know what happened. After that, I planned on retiring from my contracts and focus on growing the store.

"What I didn't know was that behind all the laundering was a bigger, more established cartel. Had I known they were involved, I would have come up with another final job. But it was the money from that final job that enabled me to buy

Charlotte her dream house, the mansion Will grew up in. That's also how I was able to later fund the building of the store that made Hargrove's into the fine department stores they are today.

"That winter's night twenty-five years ago made me realize how stupid I had been. I thought I was untouchable. Stewart had warned me about the organization and how they were after me, but I didn't listen. When everything happened and it was just a ridiculous drunk who wounded me so badly and killed the love of my life, I finally accepted I wasn't meant to be happy and that as long as I was around, Will's life would be at risk.

"When Charlotte died, I died, too. I couldn't stay. I couldn't go back to that house she loved so much, just like this was the first time I returned to the monastery. Charlotte's death turned me into a coward running from my memories.

"Eventually I did return to my old habits. It was the only way I knew how to survive. The ironic thing was my return proved to the cartel that I was still alive. Until then, Will was safe. My leaving was exactly what put him in danger, after all.

"I spent all these years searching for them. Slowly taking each of them out one by one. Dimitri and his men were the last of them. Will is safe now. He'll never be bothered again."

Walking over to Deborah and seeing how she wore her emotions in her face, I knew why Will loved her. I wondered if she knew how much she meant to him and if he knew she felt the same. I knew people. I could see it in them.

"Tell Will I love him. And when he's ready, please tell him my story. Hopefully one day he'll see fit to forgive me," I said, lowering my head.

"I will," Deborah said. "I'll tell him everything once he's ready to hear it. He just needs some time right now."

"I know. I understand. I'm glad he found someone, and maybe one day you and I will get to know each other. In the meantime, it's time for me to go. If Will ever wants to talk, Stewart knows how to reach me."

Entering the abbey, I walked with Charlotte beside me hooting and spinning in circles with her arms stretched out as she listened to the echo. She disappeared as I reached out to touch her hand. I understood Will's being haunted by our deaths more than he would ever know.

Chapter Nineteen

Deborah

After a night of bad dreams, I awoke the next morning, surprised to not find Will in bed beside me. My head felt heavy as I sat up and forced myself out of bed. I tried remembering what we did the night before, but my head hurt too much. *Guess this is what a hangover feels like.*

Finally managing to make it to the door, I stumbled a few feet then held on to the doorframe.

"Will?" I said, my voice raspy and dry. "Will? Where are you?"

"Will's gone," said a deep voice.

A chill went up my spine, raising the tiny hairs at the back of my neck. I gasped, feeling the icy clutch of fear again as yesterday rushed back to me. Reaching for the door, I tried to close it as quickly as possible but fell to the floor. As I attempted to stand, the sound of footsteps closed in so I crawled towards the bed, hoping to hide.

"Deborah, stop. You're going to get hurt," said the voice.

My heart felt like it would burst at any second. I couldn't breathe, and I shivered as a cold sweat covered my body. The room began to spin when a pair of strong hands slid under my arms and lifted me up like a rag doll.

"Please don't hurt me. I swear I don't know anything," I begged.

"Deborah, focus! It's me, Stewart. You're experiencing the aftereffects of the drug they gave you. The poison in it has a slow release."

Suddenly my vision cleared and I recognized him. Breathing a long sigh of relief and feeling weak, I let him carry me into the main room of the suite and set me down on the couch. As he entered the kitchen, I looked around for any sign of Will. I had hoped he would return to the hotel after leaving us at the monastery.

"Stewart? Where's Will? What do you mean he's gone?"

Stewart came back with a glass of something and handed it to me.

"Drink. It's not going to taste good, but this elixir will counteract the poison in your system."

I took a sip and grimaced. The elixir was thick but cold. As I drank, I felt its effects already taking over the poison in my system.

"The whole thing?" I asked as I looked at the tall glass.

"Yes, just drink. I let myself in earlier when I came looking for Will. You were up but feverish. I hoped sleep would help, but it's obvious the drug they used was meant to kill Will after they released him."

"Kill?" I took a gulp of the liquid once I realized it would save my life.

"Will left the jet, but my sources tell me he's back in Canyon Cove at King Manor."

"Why would he just leave like that? Never mind, don't answer that. I can't even begin to imagine what he's going through. For twenty-five years he thought his parents were dead, now he knows his father is still alive."

"I'm sure when he's ready, you'll hear from him," Stewart said as he took the empty glass from me. "In the meantime, try not to worry."

"Not worry? People tried to kill us yesterday and you're telling me not to worry?" I couldn't help the hysteria in my voice.

He didn't seem fazed by my tone. Looking briefly at his watch, he turned back to me. His eyes changed from calm to dangerous and then calm again, but I knew I was safe.

"As of fifteen minutes ago, the organization those men belonged to has been terminated. The bodies were discovered," he chose his words carefully as if they meant much more than they should. "Will can now lead a normal life."

Stewart looked down, his brown eyes sad, and I realized how much Will's father being alive affected him, too. Remembering how he saved us, I couldn't help but ask how much he knew. I didn't know if he would tell me, but I had to give it a shot. He knew things Will needed to know but never would.

"Stewart? You knew Bill King was alive, didn't you?"

He didn't reply. He examined my face for a moment before walking over to the large window and looking outside at the picturesque view. Rubbing his bald head as if he was pushing imaginary hair out of his eyes, he finally sat on a large chair with his back to a corner of the room.

"Yes, I knew he was alive. I've always known."

I nodded, my suspicions confirmed. It wasn't enough though. Who was this mysterious man who devoted his life to the man I loved? Looking over at him, his eyes seemed warm and welcoming, not those of the vicious killer I knew him to be. *How did he get that way?*

Chapter Twenty

Stewart

Most people don't realize how transparent they are, I thought. In the seconds an average person took to make a decision, I already knew what their choice would be and why that person chose it. That didn't make me special. It made me observant.

Deborah sat curled up on the couch, and I knew what she wanted to ask. I waited for her to ask it. All these years, I never revealed anything about myself to anyone, and I could see the gears turning in her head as she realized she could just ask me. *Do it, Deborah, ask. It really is that simple.*

"How did you get involved in all of this? You were in your twenties when you started raising Will, that means you were already..." her voice trailed off, but I knew the word she couldn't bring herself to say.

"An assassin," I said, completing her sentence.

I couldn't help but grin. It was a word that always brought a smile to my face. She nodded, her face a mixture of awe and fear.

"You realize what you're asking me can get you killed, right?"

Deborah's face went white, and for a brief moment I thought she might get sick. I knew better than to mess with someone recovering from that poison, but I couldn't resist.

"Just because I asked doesn't mean you have to tell me," she said.

I could tell she was choosing her words carefully, not wanting to scare me away even though she herself was frightened. Sinking into the chair, I smiled at her, hoping to put her at ease.

"I'm playing with you, my dear, but you are right to be concerned. A hired assassin doesn't live as long as I have without knowing how to manipulate people."

"Is that what you've done to Will? Manipulated him his whole life?" she asked, her voice rising with anger.

"No. Will has always been different. He was the closest thing I ever had as family, and his father was like a father to me. I would risk my life for the King family. And I have."

Sitting quietly for a moment, I wondered how much I should tell her. It wasn't that I didn't trust her. I learned long ago that trust wasn't as important as fear, and I knew she wouldn't speak out of fear of what I could do to her.

"You have to understand that I have never told anyone my story before, not even Bill King. Although I'm sure he knew. You see, it all started around thirty years ago, when I was eighteen. I became an assassin because of a woman."

Thirty Years Ago

Jeanne DeMarco was the prettiest girl in the neighborhood. With her long, thick black hair and sparkling blue eyes, she could command the attention of anyone in town with just a smile. Somehow I lucked out and she only had eyes for me.

I never knew my father, and when I was younger a raid on the brothel my mother and I lived in took her away from me for the rest of my life. Placed in a halfway house for kids, I learned to take care of myself. I was rude, tough, and would do anything for the love of my life, Jeanne.

"I'm graduating high school next month, and then I'm gone," Jeanne said, lying in my arms as she pushed my shaggy blond hair out of my eyes.

Every night I slipped into her bedroom and stayed over. Her parents never knew, and the halfway house didn't care what I did as long as I didn't end up in jail.

"Then we can go together. Wherever you want to go."

"No, Stewie. You don't understand. I need a better life than this shit hole."

"Please don't call me that. We can make a better life together. I'll do anything for you, Jeanne."

She sighed and rolled over, turning her back towards me. I closed the distance, pressing my body against hers and listening while her breathing slowed into the rhythmic pattern of sleep. *I have to show her I can give her a better life or I'll lose her forever,* I thought.

While Jeanne was in school the next day, I filled out job applications in the few neighborhood shops that were left. Every one of them turned me down. I was too young, too inexperienced, whatever excuses they could come up with. I knew the truth. I knew none of them wanted to hire some punk-ass kid from the halfway house. No one gave me a chance.

As I made my way to the high school to pick up Jeanne, I walked past Hargrove's. They were a small department store then, not the large fine department store chain Will inherited. That didn't happen until the flagship store was built where the old tenements once stood. One of those buildings was the halfway house I was supposed to call home.

Walking past a small window display, I noticed the jewelry department in the center of the store. It was staffed by a rickety old man with coke bottle glasses and a hump on his back. He looked like almost too easy of a mark, but when I spotted a thin gold chain with a heart dangling from it, I knew I needed to get it for my girl.

Swiping it was easy, almost the easiest grab I ever did. I felt a rush as I left the store, rubbing the gold heart in my pocket between my fingers. But as I got closer to the high school, a tall slender man with dark brown hair began walking beside me.

"For money or for your girl?" he asked as he walked beside me.

"What are you talking about, old man?"

"Don't play dumb with me, Stewart. I've been watching you for months."

"Then fuck off, you perv. You think I don't know about men like you who watch little boys?"

"Cut the act. I know you swiped that necklace for your girl. And I know she wants a better life than what's left here. I can help you with that."

"And why the hell would you do that? What do you want?"

"Because you remind me of myself when I was your age. Come with me and I'll show you what your life can be like."

School was letting out, and in the distance I easily spotted Jeanne walking down the brick steps of the school with her friends.

"She deserves better than this dump," I said quietly. "Let's go. But if you try any funny business, I swear I'll cut your balls off."

He laughed and turned up the block. I followed, trying to keep up with his long strides since he didn't bother to slow down. As he drove his large black Lincoln Continental out of the city, I realized I didn't even know his name, yet he knew mine.

"William King, by the way. By now you're wondering who I am. You can call me Bill."

We arrived at a large brick house in a suburban neighborhood. It was the biggest house I'd ever seen in person, and I found it hard to not look impressed. Inside, Bill showed me to his office, where a huge wooden desk dominated the room. Taking a picture frame off his desk, he perched himself on the edge and handed the photo to me.

"That's my Jeanne. Her name is Charlotte. She's not like us and would never understand the life we grew up in."

I looked at the picture of the happy couple holding a baby. She had the same eyes as Jeanne, and I couldn't help but let my guard down a little.

"You're nothing like me, man."

"Shut up and listen. I know you've had it rough. I'm not denying you that. But I know how you think. And I think I can train you."

"Train me for what?"

"Do you want to make a lot of money? Give that girl a better life?"

"Yes, I already said that. I'd do anything for her."

"The military has a strict training method that only a few are welcomed into and even less pass. I graduated from their elite system with honors. I'm leaving that business. Charlotte and Will deserve better, and I believe the store is the way to do that."

"What's that got to do with me? Just spill it, man."

He gave me a cross look, and I felt the icy grip of fear around my heart. Suddenly I understood what he was suggesting.

"I'm willing to train you the way I was trained. I need someone who can learn how the new cartel thinks and see when we can take advantage of their situation. You're going to help me with my last job and then protect my family. In exchange, I'll make you richer than you can imagine. You're still just a child--"

"I'm not a kid, I'm eighteen. I'm not even in high school anymore."

"Dropping out of school doesn't make you an adult. I'll make you into a man you can be proud of. One your girl won't look down on like she does now."

I stood up and got in his face. Bill wasn't disturbed at all and shoved me hard on my chest, forcing me back into the chair.

"You'll work for me," he said. "People will think you're my driver while I train you in the arts and methods that will help protect my family from harm. You'll be well compensated, but no one must know exactly what you do. No one. Understand?"

I nodded. I understood more than he could imagine.

That night, I entered Jeanne's window like I always did. She sat at her desk writing and didn't turn around when I entered.

"I did it, Jeanne. I found a way for us to get out of here. I'm going to make a great life for you," I said.

She didn't turn around at first. Instead, she shook her head slowly until she smiled sadly at me.

"Let's go to bed," she said.

Present Day

"I never saw her again. She left in the middle of the night while I was deeply asleep."

"Oh Stewart, that's so sad," Deborah said, now sitting at the edge of her seat with her face in her hands.

"Turns out what she was writing when I arrived was a letter to me. She met someone else, someone she thought would be able to help her get the life she wanted. And he convinced her they had to leave right away."

"Did you ever look for her?"

"No," I said quietly. "I finally accepted she didn't want me. She might have loved me, but I guess sometimes love isn't enough."

Chapter Twenty-One

Deborah

Alone in the suite after Stewart left, I knocked on Dianna's door, needing to talk. I heard a bit of a commotion on the other side of the door, then a male voice and a woman giggling. *Did she change rooms without telling me?*

Dianna opened the door a crack, her hair disheveled with a sheet wrapped around her body. My mouth dropped open in surprise.

"I know, I know!" she said as she pushed me further into my room and closed the door behind her. "We met yesterday. His name is Jean-Marc and I swear I'm already in love."

"Well, that explains that giant smile on your face," I said laughing. "I just never thought you were such a slut!"

"Slut? Me? No! I followed the three-date rule. We had lunch together, then dinner, and then drinks. See, three." She raised her brows at me and giggled again.

"Where did you meet him? Last I saw, you were surrounded by models."

"He came to our room. He's a design assistant for Gucci and they sent him out to do some grunt work, but he needed to borrow something. We just clicked. Even if we can't understand everything we say to each other. Hmm, maybe that's why we clicked," she said before bursting into laughter.

"I'll try to not keep you away for too long, but I wanted to talk to you about work."

"He has to leave soon anyway, they have a lot of work to do, too. Plus I can't wait to hear about your day with Will."

"That's the thing, Dianna, it was the worst day of my life."

I broke into tears I didn't realize were waiting at the surface. Dianna tried to hug me while still holding onto her sheet. The sight of her waddling towards me, one arm outstretched, made me laugh, ending my tears. Quickly telling her what I thought I could, I explained the day's events.

"And now Will is gone. He's back in Canyon Cove and I can't think about anything else but going to him. He needs me. I know it."

"And what about the show? This was your dream and you worked so hard on it," she said.

"I know, and I'm torn, but to be honest I almost don't care. He means more to me than the show. I did it once, I can do it again. I'll get another show."

"Sure you won't regret leaving?"

"Right now when I think about staying, I see myself regretting not being with him."

"Then you know what to do."

She was right. I did know what to do. I had to be with him. Even if being with him only meant waiting for him to open up again.

"He left the jet. I'll ask Stewart about getting it ready so we can go. At least you'll get to ride on the fancy jet."

"Thanks Deb, but I'm going to stay. I have my plane ticket and I don't mind slumming it on a commercial line. I need to see where things go with Jean-Marc. I've never met anyone else like him."

"Well, I'm going to need details," I said jokingly, echoing what she said to me the day before. "Call me when you get back. I know I don't have to tell you to have fun."

"You know it!" she said as she grinned widely and waved before heading back through the door to her bedroom.

I heard giggling then squealing almost immediately and laughed as I distanced myself as much as possible from her door.

***

Stewart was able to get the jet ready for us to leave later that day. As I sat in my seat across the aisle from him, I wondered where I was going to go once we got back. I didn't have my apartment, and all my things were at Will's.

"You look like you have something on your mind," Stewart said as he closed his eyes and leaned his chair back.

I sighed. "Yes, I do. You brought all my things to the house. What if Will doesn't want me there anymore? I just realized I don't have anyplace to go."

"I know Will better than anyone, Deborah. I also know you feel closer to him because of everything you both went through. I'm sure he feels the same."

"Yes, but--"

"But," he said, interrupting me, "just because you haven't heard from him doesn't mean he's not thinking of you. Trust me on that."

It was hard to not trust anything Stewart said. While normally a man of few words, he never said anything unless it was true. Although Will's father made the wrong choice of abandoning his son, despite his reasons, I definitely thought he made a good decision when it came to who raised him. Stewart was a dangerous man, but at his core he was one of the best men I knew.

***

It was late when we finally landed at the Canyon Cove airport, and I couldn't help but think about my cat Trap and wonder how he was doing with Ashley and Xander. I sent her a text figuring that if she was asleep she wouldn't respond until morning, but instead she called me back.

"Hello? Ashley?"

"You sound surprised," she said as she laughed.

"I was worried it was too late. It's 10pm and you have a baby."

"Exactly, I have a baby. That means I don't sleep. I'm kidding, but seriously, I've always been a night owl. Ten is too early for sleep. Is everything okay? I didn't expect to hear from you while you were away."

"I just got back. I'm actually still on the plane. I was wondering how Trap was doing without me."

"He's great. I'm not sure he even realizes you're gone."

"Damn cat. That sounds about right," I said, laughing.

"What's really going on, Deborah? You're home early, Fashion Week hasn't even started, and all you're talking about is your cat. I'm not stupid."

"Fine, yes, you're right. I just...don't want to go home just yet. That's all."

"Come over. I'll make some hot chocolate and you can stay in the guest room and take Trap home in the morning."

"You sure? I don't want to intrude. It's late."

"It's not that late and I could use the company. Xander had to go away overnight on business."

"Okay, I'll see you soon then."

***

As I turned onto the gravel driveway of the Boone's home, I was surprised by how noisy it was. If they weren't awake before, I definitely woke them now. Ashley stepped out of the old Georgian mansion with a large blue crocheted blanket wrapped around her shoulders and her dark hair pulled back into a ponytail.

"Hurry up!" she said. "I'm already heating up the milk."

I followed her through the house to the long kitchen where she turned off the stove and portioned the milk into a couple of large mugs before dropping pieces of chocolate inside.

"This was how my mom used to make it when I was real little," she said, smiling. "I'm trying to redo all the things I remember fondly of her."

As I sat down at the kitchen table, I felt the familiar nudge of Trap against my leg and reached down to pet him.

"Spill, Deb. What's going on?"

"It's so complicated, I really don't know what to say."

"What's complicated?"

"Will. Paris. Now. I don't even know if he wants to see me. For all I know, he wants nothing to do with me. I mean it's okay, I'm not going to go psycho or anything. I respect his decision, but I just wish I knew what to do."

"You're really not making any sense. Back up."

I told Ashley how Will gave me my own room in his mansion and how I let go of my apartment and moved all my things there. Then I told her a brief version of the trip, steering clear from giving her too many details and focusing on Will's departure almost two days ago.

"That's pretty much everything. I guess I just don't feel comfortable showing up at his house when he couldn't even be bothered to leave a note to say goodbye. What if things have changed?"

"Then don't. Stay here as long as you want to. But can I say something?" I nodded to answer her before she continued. "If you really love him, you should go to him. You don't know what he's going through right now. He might think he wants no one around, but I bet that'll change once he sees you came back early. Have you tried calling him?"

"No," I said softly. "I was afraid he'd tell me to fuck off."

"Listen, I don't know exactly what you've been through, but the Deborah I know is the one who tells people to fuck off, not the other way around. Sleep here tonight, but I really think you should see him in the morning. It's the only way you'll know for sure what he's really thinking."

Ashley was right. I wasn't acting like myself. I didn't know if it was the trauma of the kidnapping or the residual effects of the drug, but I needed to move on from this selfishness and be there for the man I loved. First thing in the morning, I would head over to King Manor and find him.

Chapter Twenty-Two

Deborah

I left Ashley's in the morning, ready to face whatever might happen at Will's. I couldn't avoid it any longer, and I didn't want to. It was time to see how he really was doing and see how I could help, if he would let me. Unsure what to expect, my hands felt moist and my stomach turned a little, but I wasn't going to back down.

Slowing down at the entrance, I was surprised to find the gate wide open. My first thought was of the men who kidnapped us in Paris, and I worried for Will's safety as I felt a chill overtake me again.

The loud honk behind me startled me out of my fear and back to the King Manor driveway. I quickly moved my car over to the side as a plumbing truck drove past.

"That's odd. I wonder what's going on," I said out loud.

As I reached the circular part of the driveway with the fountain, I couldn't believe how many trucks were there. Parking closer to the garden than the house, I surveyed each of the trucks as I tried to guess why they were there but couldn't come up with anything.

Walking up the path to the house, I noticed a man in jeans and a button shirt directing the contractors to different locations on the first floor and outside.

"Excuse me," I said as I tapped his shoulder, hoping to find out where Will was.

"Deborah!" Will exclaimed as he turned around. "I was hoping you'd come home."

He picked me up and spun me around then kissed me after dipping me back, leaving me breathless and woozy.

"What's going on here? And where's your suit?" I said, teasing him.

"Come, walk with me," he said, slipping his arm around my shoulders and pressing me against him. "I want to show you something."

We walked past the gardens and towards the furthest part of the property, away from the mansion. Following a stone path that curved through the fields, I wondered where he was taking me.

"After everything that happened in Paris, I had to leave. I needed to get as far away as possible. I'm sorry I didn't say anything. I needed some time alone to think about things."

"I figured that's what happened, Will. But I was still really worried."

"I know. And for that, I apologize. My whole life came into question. Everything I believed about my father was wrong. All this time I thought he was dead, I remembered his words to live life without regrets and I did the complete opposite. I hid away, not wanting to feel loss again. I let the danger he put me in rule everything I did. Instead of living without regrets, I regretted not only everything I did but even the things I didn't do." He stopped and turned to look into my eyes. "That is, until I met you.

"That first day I saw you in the store changed everything for me. Suddenly I wanted to live, to be a part of something. You were so full of life it was contagious. I began changing things, and letting myself be vulnerable to you was one of them.

"When you got upset on the plane, I almost came home. I realized how hard everything was and I didn't want to deal with it. It was easier to hide and be alone, but I realized I'd regret it if I never spent another minute with you, so I waited for you to stop being so stubborn and realize what happened wasn't that big of a deal. Even if I was wrong and should have told you exactly who I was," he said with a lopsided grin.

"Jeez, if this is an apology, I think it needs some work," I said, grinning back at him.

"Just listen to me. I took that commercial flight back instead of my jet because I didn't want to be Will King for once. I just wanted to be like everyone else. What I saw while I waited were families and couples. I watched how they were with each other, and I understood that my father faking his death wasn't a selfish act like I first thought, he did it because it was the only way he knew how to protect me. He had just lost his wife and didn't want to lose his son, too.

"The ironic thing is what he did kept me from having my own love. But I didn't realize I was missing that until I met you."

We arrived at a large clearing where bulldozers and other construction vehicles were digging and moving dirt around as they flattened the area. Behind the clearing was the gentle slope of the lush green valley just beginning to change colors for fall, and in the distance I could see the ocean.

"Oh wow, what a gorgeous view!" I said. "What's going on here?"

"The night I lost my parents, my father wanted to show me my future. He said that future was Hargrove's and he was right. If it wasn't for Hargrove's and that particular store, I would have never met you."

Will took both my hands into his as he spoke. The world stood still as I listened to him intently over the noise of the construction, lost in the glittering green flecks of his eyes.

"You are my future, Deborah Hansen. In the past two days I've been home, I've begun transforming the original mansion and the grounds surrounding it into an art museum to show off all of my mother's collections. I also started this," he said as he waved his hand to point to the construction. "I only have preliminary sketches so they can begin clearing the land, but I want us to design a home together for us to live in. It can have whatever we want. If you want a design studio, then we can build one there, too."

"I...I don't know what to say--"

"Don't say anything at all, I'm not done. You are incredible, you know that? I love how you're so passionate about things that you can sometimes get irrational and crazy. I love how you're so stubborn that even though you know you're being a little nutty, you won't apologize for it."

"Umm, I'm not sure I like where this is going," I said as I crossed my arms in front of me.

He laughed and took my hands back and held them. "Bear with me. I'm not used to talking about my feelings."

"Okay then, keep talking."

"See, right there. I love how your brow furrows whenever you're not sure about something. Or how every single thought is reflected on your face. I love how you know you're talented but refuse to accept it at the same time. And I love your body, your curves, your softness."

He lowered himself down on one knee as he looked up at me. Letting go of my hands, he reached into his jeans pocket and pulled out a small Tiffany ring box. My hands flew to my open mouth in surprise as I held my breath while Will opened the box. It was the longest two seconds of my life.

The ring had an oval deep blue sapphire surrounded by a halo of small glittering diamonds. It was set in platinum and sparkled as if it had a life all its own.

"My world began when you entered it and it would end if you left it. I can't imagine my life without you. Deborah, I love you. Will you marry me?"

"Yes, oh yes!" I said as I wrapped my arms around him, knocking him off balance. "I love you too, Will. Oh my God, yes!"

He laughed and kissed me, making my heart pound wildly in my chest.

"I went shopping for it as soon as I got home. I know it's not a traditional engagement ring, but as soon as I saw it, I knew you would love it."

"You're right, it's the most gorgeous ring I've ever seen. It's absolutely amazing!"

I admired the ring as we sat on the ground in front of where our new home would one day stand. The sun caught the blue stone and reminded me of my ocean blue chiffon gown. I made the right decision coming home, but if I could be in two places at once, I would. Will leaned back as he examined my face, his head tilted.

"Wait a second. What about Paris? I never meant for you to come home early," he said.

"I was worried about you. I couldn't stay without knowing how you were. You went through a lot. We went through a lot in our short time out there. I don't know that I could do my best with the collection if my head was out here with you."

"Then you have to go back. Take the jet. I couldn't forgive myself if you let your dream go because of me."

"I don't have time to do all the alterations. Even with Dianna still out there, I have my samples here."

"Then find another assistant. Surely between the three of you, you can do it. I'll call Mimi and see if I can get your slot switched."

My mind raced. *Another assistant?* The only other person I really knew was Ashley, and she couldn't fly out to Paris with me. *But wait, maybe...*

I pulled out my cell phone and found the number I had added just a few weeks ago. Joshua Cane was my only hope.

"Hi, Joshua. It's Deborah Hansen. I don't know if you remember me, but--"

"Of course I remember you, sweetheart. I've been keeping tabs on you since we met. How's Paris?"

"I'm in Canyon Cove."

"Did something happen?"

"Yes and no. It's a long story. I need a favor that involves you flying with me back to Paris today. Any chance you can get away and help me out? You did say us designers needed to stick together."

"Sweetie, you had me at Paris. Give me a couple of hours to take care of things here. We'll make sure your designs look fabulous on that runway."

***

Will was able to get me a one-day extension because another designer dropped out due to time constraints. Joshua and I worked the entire flight using Dianna's measurements, but it still wasn't enough. We made alterations all the way to just before the show. While Dianna took care of planning hair, makeup, and accessories for the models, Joshua and I finished any last minute fixes right on the models as they wore the clothes.

In the end, the models looked perfect and no one had any idea that we took it down to the wire. Dianna, Joshua, and I watched the show from a backstage monitor. The models worked it on the runway. Just like Joshua foretold, they looked fabulous.

As I watched the models strut down the runway, I couldn't tear my eyes away from them. The clothing looked even better than I ever imagined. I had a permanent smile on my face and the day would have been perfect if Will had been there with me.

We only had enough models for my original collection, but I couldn't let my new design go ignored. Knowing that as the designer I'd be going down the runway, I wore the Eiffel Tower inspired cream-colored dress. The last model wore my ocean blue chiffon gown and as she came back up the runway, I stepped out and walked with her as we led the rest of the models back out. The crowd applauded as my models lined up.

Looking out at the faceless crowd for a moment, I thought about how lucky I was that I didn't fall on my face as I walked with the models. That was all I needed, to become fashion roadkill at my first show.

Before turning back, the model next to me bent down closer to my level and pointed into the crowd. I looked where she pointed and had to blink in disbelief. Will sat in the crowd next to Amanda Cunning and Tim Ross, and the three of them rose to their feet as they clapped. Humbled, I lowered my head and curtsied, thanking them from afar. It was my dream come true.

Chapter Twenty-Three

Deborah

The sun beat down, barely giving any escape even under the trees. Looking at the old brick campus buildings I had my classes in, I couldn't believe I was back at graduation just a year later. Wearing the black cap and gown again, this time with a different sash over my shoulders, I sat on a white wooden folding chair just off the side of the stage.

Will sat beside me in a tan suit with a green print tie that matched the flecks in his hazel eyes. As he held my hand, I couldn't help but admire my engagement ring. It didn't matter how many months I had worn it, the way the light caught the circle of diamonds around the large deep blue sapphire always took my breath away.

Joshua Cane took the stage wearing a black cap and gown with the same sash I had over my shoulders. He winked in my direction as he approached the podium and smiled at the audience.

"At this time last year, I had the opportunity to meet today's honoree, Deborah Hansen. I recognized her talent and practically begged her to work for me. She turned me down. Luckily for everyone else, she knew she was destined for better things.

"Deborah has a way of endearing herself to people. It's in her smile, her personality, and her drive. She chased her dream by taking a job at Hargrove's and won the opportunity to show an original collection at Fashion Week in Paris, a feat many designers dream of but never reach.

"So you can imagine my surprise when Deborah called me, home early from Paris after an emergency, and asked if I would fly back to Paris with her. Deborah is the most hardworking and creative person I have ever had the pleasure of working with. And it's because of our mutual work ethic that a partnership was born.

"But I'm not here to talk about our success though. I'm here to talk about Deborah's.

"In the past year, Deborah has had her first collection at Fashion Week, opened Hansen + Cane with her very handsome design partner, started her own line exclusively sold at Hargrove's fine department stores, and has been so busy she's been forced to turn down design requests from some of the hottest movie and music stars.

"As if that wasn't enough, she was also instrumental in the creation of the Working Designer Grant for students like herself who have no choice but to juggle both work and school.

"To honor all of her hard work, I'm here to present Deborah with an honorary degree for her incredible devotion to the art of fashion design. Everyone, please put your hands together for one of my dearest friends and business partners, Miss Deborah Hansen." Joshua stepped back from the podium, clapping.

Humbled and embarrassed, I slowly rose from my seat while everyone clapped. I climbed the stage, not very different from last year when I got my diploma, but feeling so much more confident and happy.

My heart raced in my chest knowing I needed to say a few words. Hugging Joshua, I took a deep breath before turning around and facing the large crowd of students, their families and friends, and the school administrators. I looked down at Will and smiled back at him, feeling better as I nervously spun my engagement ring around my finger.

"Thank you for this incredible honor. I can't help but think the school ran out of people to give this to," I said as the crowd laughed politely. After taking another deep breath, I continued. "I want to dedicate this honorary degree to my grandmother. If it wasn't for her endless support and patience, I would've never been able to achieve the things I've done."

In the distance I heard a rumble of thunder and smiled, knowing my grandma was watching over me as she had been since her death. I knew she'd be proud of all my successes if she had been alive to see them. I also knew she would love Will as much as I did.

Missing her, my eyes filled with tears as they always did when I thought about her too much. I blinked, trying to hold the tears back as my vision blurred. After swallowing hard, I forced a smile.

"I'm really no good at this and no one wants to hear a long speech, so really, from the bottom of my heart, thank you."

The crowd applauded again as I walked off the stage and back to my seat next to Will, who hugged me and held out a handkerchief. I couldn't help but laugh when I saw it, making the tears finally flow down my cheeks.

Will gently wiped my tears with the handkerchief then kissed my forehead. Moving closer to me, he put his arm around my shoulders and I leaned into him.

"I'm so proud of you, Deborah. There's just one small thing."

"Is something wrong?"

"Yes, there is. You see, I have this suit that needs to be tailored, and I'm still waiting for you to show me that new method of measuring my inseam."

He grinned that same lopsided, knowing grin from the first day we met. His eyes twinkled mischievously and I laughed, surprised he remembered that. I had to be the luckiest woman alive. Not only did I have my dream job, but I had my very own Mr. Sexy who wanted to be with me forever.

No Regrets Bonus Scene

"Let's go, Deborah," Ashley said as she walked ahead of me through the parking lot. "I can't believe we're going to be late."

Mirabella's Café was on the corner of a strip mall in downtown Canyon Cove. Golden light spilled onto the sidewalk from the restaurant's large windows, and inside I could see that everyone else was already there.

"I told you, it doesn't matter what I do, I'm always late," I said.

"How is this possible? I picked you up so you wouldn't be late."

"You used to be late all the time too, remember? I think you caught my lateness."

"Hmm, so lateness is a virus," Ashley said with a grin. "I buy it."

The bells hanging from the door jingled as

Ashley pulled the door open. The scent of cinnamon rolls, one of Mirabella's specialties, wafted towards me as we walked through the café to the round table we always sat at.

We had started going to Mirabella's months ago as a way to force ourselves to never lose touch. If I remembered correctly, Jackie, Ashley's old friend, was the first to come up with the idea to get Ashley out of the house after the baby was born. As time went on, we added more friends until there were seven of us.

"It's about time," Jackie said. "We're starving. I hope you don't mind, we ordered some appetizers a few minutes ago."

"No, that's great," Ashley said. "It seems I caught Deborah's lateness."

"I don't know," Samantha said. "I think Deborah might have caught that from you."

"Mental note, do not show up late," Becca said with a laugh.

"Actually, Becca, you're the reason we're late," I teased.

"Me? What did I do?"

"I was waiting for Will to come home, but he got held up in a board meeting for the South End restoration project. Eventually Ashley and I left before he got back."

"Mmm, yeah, sorry about that. The meeting went longer than planned. I would've been late if I didn't work a couple blocks away."

"It's really great how so many people are coming together to fix that area up," Ashley said.

"Will was excited when he heard about it," I said. "After what happened to his parents, he'll do anything he can to prevent that from happening to someone else."

"And how is Mr. Sexy?" Tara asked.

"He's just amazing," I said. "He's been so supportive of my work with Joshua and…he just makes me so happy. I feel stupid sometimes because I'm always smiling. What about you and Mason? Anything new there?"

Tara sighed. "I'm going to do it. I said yes to a date and I swear I will not cancel this time."

"You have so much history together, Tara," Ashley said. "And it's obvious you still have feelings for him."

"I've never gotten over him," she said. "Seeing him, talking to him, brings all of that back."

Tara looked down and it was clear she didn't want to talk about it anymore. As Samantha pulled out her phone to show off some baby pictures, my phone chimed in my bag. I pulled it out and saw a text from Will.

> Will: *Any chance I can steal you away?*
> Me: *Maybe. What did you have in mind?*
> Will: *I was thinking dinner at The Breezes. We haven't been there since our first date.*
> Me: *I can't believe you remember that.*
> Will: *I remember everything. Is that a yes?*

I looked up at my friends and felt torn. Cassie, Ashley's cousin, was sitting next to me. She must have seen the look on my face because she leaned towards me.

"Something wrong?" she asked.

I showed her Will's texts and whispered so no one else would hear. "I don't know what to do. I know I see him all the time and you guys maybe once a month, but..."

"If Gabriel sent me that text, I'd go. Sometimes you can't listen to what your head is saying, you have to go with your heart."

I nodded. She was right. And while I loved my friends, I couldn't pass up Will wanting to take me to the place where we had our first date. I knew

I'd regret that if I did, so I texted him back then waited for a lull in the conversation.

"Umm, I'm sorry, but I think I need to go," I said.

"So soon? Is everything okay?" Ashley asked.

"Everything's fine. Will texted me and wants to take me to The Breezes, where we had our first date."

"Ooh, nice," Jackie said. "Go, we'll expect details next time though."

I hugged them all good-bye and as I stepped out onto the sidewalk, Will pulled up. My heart thumped in my chest like it did the first time I saw him. I got into the car and his hand reached for the back of my neck and pulled me close as he claimed my lips with his.

"Wow, what was that for?" I asked, a little out of breath.

"That was for my beautiful wife. I just wanted to make sure you know I love you," he said, his eyes a little sad.

"I love you too. Is everything okay? I thought you were just at a meeting."

"I was. And then I drove past where my mother died and I thought about how short life is.

You never know when something is going to happen, good or bad. So I want to make a promise to you. I promise that every day I will make sure you know how much I love you. I couldn't imagine something happening and being left wondering if you knew how much you mean to me. You are my everything."

He took my hand and intertwined his fingers with mine then smiled at me. I wanted to tell him how much he meant to me too, but he left me speechless. He put the car in gear and started to drive.

"So, The Breezes?" he asked.

"Let's just go home."

"Are you sure? I thought you might like a fancy dinner."

"Only if that's what you really want. I just want to spend time with you."

He squeezed my hand and we drove towards home. Will and I had been through many things in our short time together, but one thing I knew for sure was that we both loved each other very much and always would. He was more than just my Mr. Sexy, he was my Mr. Everything.

About The Author

Liliana Rhodes is a New York Times and USA Today Bestselling Author who writes Contemporary and Paranormal Romance. Blessed with an overactive imagination, she is always writing and plotting her next stories. She enjoys movies, reading, photography, and listening to music. After growing up in New Jersey, Liliana now lives in California with her husband, son, two dogs who are treated better than some people, and two parrots who plan to take over the world.

Connect Online

www.LilianaRhodes.com

www.facebook.com/AuthorLilianaRhodes

Made in the USA
Middletown, DE
21 June 2018